GIDEON'S CUBE

THE CHRONICALS OF GIDEON SPENCER

BY

MICHAEL E. MORGAN

GIDEON'S CUBE
THE CHRONICLES OF GIDEON SPENCER

Copyright © 2023 by Michael E. Morgan

For information write to:

Dawntrader Books, LLC
34522 N Scottsdale Rd.
P.O. Box D120 - 413
Scottsdale, Arizona
85331

If you are unable to order this book from your local bookseller, or Amazon.com, you may order directly from the publisher.
Quantity discounts for organizations are available.

Edited by Joe Pierce

Cover and book design by
Michael E. Morgan

Publisher's Cataloging-in-Publication Data
ISBN 978-0990-313-366

10 9 8 7 6 5 4 3 2 1

By the year 2256, the solar system comprised several colonized planets which included Mars, Venus and Jupiter. The Lunar Station became the first base of translunar operations in the latter part of the 21st century. The mining of raw materials on otherworlds, including large asteroids in the outer Kuyper belt, began by the year 2157.

By 2128, the population on earth had grown to 12.8 billion. Life on the surface was no longer workable. Severe weather, global drought and frigid temperatures made surface living intolerable. After the plague of 2129, over two-thirds of the total population perished. The spread of the plague was out of control.

The atmosphere became toxic in many places, with an aerial dispersion of genetically created anti-viral agents to halt the spread. The rest of humanity sought the unused deep underground facilities.

The military built these in the early 21st century, originally to provide shelter for government officials and key personnel in the event of a thermonuclear conflict. These underground facilities, called Dumbs (deep underground military bases) became the last refuge where small hovels of humanity survived. Cottage industries still operated there with reasonable safety, but suffered from very limited production efforts.

Terraforming other planets with fusion powered scrubbers coupled with FTL (faster than light) drive transport technology provided efficient human migration to these other planetary systems, the earth, left behind declining into a planetary wasteland.

The FTL Lyle Drive, invented by Dr. Joseph Lyle in 2149, made the first real migration to Mars a reality, offering those who wanted off planet a new life.

For hundreds of earth years, scientists believed the asteroid belt formed from the primordial nebula. Later on, the Coalition of Planets Science team conducted extensive investigations, which revealed evidence that led to the truth. A rogue planet streamed into the inner solar system millions of years in the past, from somewhere out in the Kuyper and or Oort Cloud, a larger ring of comets and other space debris extending well beyond the solar system.

Originally, a large planet in the fifth orbit, called Tiamat, collided with the rogue planet. Forces have destroyed much of Tiamat, leaving one sizeable chunk to drift out of the fifth orbit and into the third orbit around the sun. It also drew millions of years of ice comets containing trillions of deciliters of frozen water into the area of impact. Those also drifted into the third orbit close behind. They melted because of the heat in the closer orbit and collectively formed the rest of Tiamat into a sphere made mostly of liquid water called the Earth. The remains of Tiamat in the fifth orbit left behind to form the Asteroid belt.

The belt is a ring-shaped area in the Solar System, between the orbits of the planets Jupiter and Mars. All sizes of irregularly shaped solid bodies lie within the ring, much smaller than planets, though they are called asteroids; They classified some as planetoids. Their spectra categorize individual asteroids within the asteroid belt, with most falling into three basic groups: carbonaceous (C-type), silicate (S-type), and metal-rich (M-type).

The inner belt comprised several of the largest planetoids, including Ceres, Vesta, Pallas, and Hygeia. Also, there was Berenger Station, a large orbiting satellite representing the independent mining headquarters for the belt, parked in a geosynchronous orbit around Ceres.

We refer this belt to the main belt, different from other asteroid populations in the Solar System. The asteroid Ceres is large enough to be a dwarf planet and is about 950 km in diameter. Vesta, Pallas, and Hygeia have mean diameters of less than 600 km. Most of the asteroid material in the belt is so fine that early unmanned spacecraft traversed it without incident.

***

As Martian colonies grew larger into stable communities, mining operations became the primary staple of the Martian economy. Food and water to support these colonies soon became a very expensive commodity to the inhabitants.

The Planetary Mining Consortium (PMC) or the Mining Alliance became the single resource for those colonies. The concept of the 'company store, a legendary earth term began by the poor, described the harsh coal mining operations of Appalachia during the 20th century. Corrupt coal syndicates brutalized miners in the deep south during that period. Coal and crude oil production finally gave way to the 'green economy' but that program collapsed after the global climate degraded significantly.

It again rekindled unfair management practices off world, enslaving desperate settlers on Mars and Venus, forcing them to work the mines just for food and water. In addition, the Alliance also controlled the housing and rebreathing apparatus and shielded garments required for some of the work.

These precious commodities were on loan only. The company offered these tools and clothing for rental fees against credit for work performed. This would create a permanent indebtedness, to ensure worker devotion to their job. Refusal of the offer would cause their immediate dismissal. Then the Alliance would simply recruit another to take their place.

Once FTL drives became a common mode of transport, Mars became the 'gold coast' outpost for all goods and services throughout the solar system. Besides the regular trade routes, stable wormhole development created the possibility of exploring beyond the solar system into other parts of the galaxy.

The Martian colonies became the first mining operations under the Mining Alliance. Soon, mining operations extended to the moons Europa, Calisto and Io.

Later, the outer belt colonies formed on the asteroids of Ceres with Berenger Station as their satellite headquarters. These brave independents sought fame and fortune and refuge from the overbearing mining Alliance. These rebellious and independent groups eventually formed a separate mining consortium.

***

Berenger Station resembled a fortress in space. The last area before the outer system with an atmosphere. Its ten-kilometer diameter was armored and reinforced with six-meter thick Void steel panels.

Jutting from the station's center is an enormous toroidal ring. The outer structure is a bifurcated cylinder, big enough to be called a planetoid and small enough to be called a floating city. It travels a diagonal orbit around Ceres, with each rotation taking about twenty-five minutes. Etched into its surface is a ring of docking ports, with mining ships docked at each port.

Inside, the toroid reeked of ozone and metal. Air is thin and cold, walls are cool to the touch. Walls are razor sharp in places and smooth in others. The floors are cool to the feet and walls are barren of fixtures or any way to secure oneself. The space station feels like steel, cold and hard under your boots. Your palm glides across the surface, almost too smooth to be real.

Well-organized pirates directed from Berenger, armed with pulse weapons and small scouts, FTL Rasors, easily out maneuvered company cargo cruisers. They began raiding mineral transports from Mars. As Alliance profits plunged, the Mining Alliance brought in mercenary marshals to engage with the bandits attempting to curb theefforts.

The bad feelings among the miner population began with open complaints about high rents deducted against their earnings and the lack of safety in their work environment. Regular work strikes occurred to threaten Alliance management with hopes to urge them to the negotiating table. Continued minor skirmishes between the Alliance marshals and miners eventually sped up into larger and more destructive events until a rebellion formed the terrorist group called the Red Sword.

Then an organized uprising began at Berenger Station. The company brought in marshals hoping to suppress the rising tide of rebellion. The marshals underestimated the strength of the pirate supported group. Pirate raiders easily dodged the marshal's assaults. Then suddenly they appeared to disband and disperse, only to expand their efforts deeper into other mining operations, stirring miners to support their actions and philosophy.

Federal Military Rangers enlarged the mercenary's ranks later. They attacked well-known pirate strongholds. Eventually, these minor skirmishes only imbedded the pirate raiders deeper into the other mining colonies.

The raiders continued with a program of efficient hit-and-run tactics. Sometimes, the scale of their attacks escalated into major conflicts. They brought in several Federal Ranger troop ships to destroy the renegade pirate bases with a single blow. That effort failed, leading to open warfare for years between ex-miner raiders, company marshals and federal Rangers.

The conflict continued with powerful feelings amongst the colonists. They wanted to defend against the Alliance presence favoring a strong sense of Martian Sovereignty. Then the nature of the war changed. No longer a war about socio-economic differences, but a war for independence for Mars and the Martian colonies as well as, other colonist communities sympathetic to the Martian cause in the asteroid belt and the outer Kuyper belt.

The outer mining colonies beyond Mars, Venus and Jupiter were independent from the mining consortium. Though the consortium tolerated their independence, the consortium was constantly trying to disrupt their mining operations through intimidation and sabotage tactics, curbing their profits and slowing down production. The Alliance constantly encouraged them to give up their independent operations and join the consortium.

***

Life in the solar system of Sol continued as a microcosm of physical reality, a fledgling of organic life completely unaware, ignorant of the sinister greater reality of the Dark Empire, content to live life with the myths and legends of the Gods and the promise of divine providence.

Eons ago, the Dark Empire had begun in the farthest reaches of the universe, far outside the Sol solar system, beginning as a minor force in a minor 'universe' controlled by a major galactic power. Because of their success in conquering their own universe, they soon became the major galactic power and began conquering other 'universes,' spreading their version of peace through conquest and death. The Dark Empire considered themselves the 'descendants' of a long-dead, but 'magnificent' race of beings simply referred to as the 'Cycle'.

They considered themselves the 'heirs' to the legacy of that ancient dead race, and they harbored a jealous obsession with the thought of their ancestors, who had created this 'universe' and all that was in it, and had abandoned it. The Dark Empire desired to destroy life, to create a winter and return this 'universe' to a state of frozen lifelessness. They desired to steal the heat, the light, and the life of every living thing.

The stars in the Sol solar system shined as they have since their birth. Totally unaware of the Dark Empire's hidden presence. The Empire gave the order that the black fleet would visit all systems in the Milky Way galaxy. They would then accomplish total domination.

The black fleet moved slowly from one star to the next and from one system to the next in their black polished ships. They moved slowly, with calculated energy. In their minds was a mission any previous race in the known universe had never accomplished before, the likes of which, certainly not by a race so evil.

Anyone of the crew of these ships that the Emperor's Black Guard immediately eliminated harbored thoughts of pity or weakness. The black fleet moved into the Orion arm of the Milky Way galaxy. Soon, the Dark Empire consumed and assimilated the Orion system, continuing to grow stronger....and then came the shadow of war.

The Dark Emperor and his vast legions unleashed the most devastating weapon of war when they prepared to invade the solar system of Sol, a system of light, hope, and peacefulness.

Unbeknownst to the solar system, one of the Dark Lord in charge of capturing planets had been a little careless. He had been called to appear before the Dark Emperor to answer for his mistakes. Upon appearing before him, the Dark Emperor punished the Dark Lord.

The Dark Emperor, being omnipotent and all knowing, had seen the future, and dispatched the Dark Lord to the physical dimension in which still existed. When the Dark Lord found himself in this dimension, he plotted his revenge. He spent his time plotting, planning, and brooding, trying to devise a way to escape the Dark Emperor's wrath. He finally came up with the perfect plan: if he could not escape the Dark Emperor, he would escape the physical dimension, and if he could not escape the physical dimension, he would escape the Dark Empire. It was a risky plan, but it was the only one that he could think of.

He spent many eons in this dimension toying with people, causing mayhem and tormenting them throughout the many worlds. He had a knack for peeking into other dimensions and found out about the ancient Zodiac War. Now, since his falsely sworn allegiance to the Dark Emperor, he has become the mastermind behind the plans of the Dark Emperor.

When the Dark Emperor imprisoned the Dark Lord in the limitations of the physical dimension, the Dark Lord used his magic to blind the Dark Emperor temporarily from the physical realm, and established the Council of 9 to rule in his place. He withdrew from the physical world, and focused on preparing a way to deliver his final vengeance, the complete takeover of the Dark Empire.

In the meantime, the Council of 9 established a different way. They created laws that would govern all civilizations in the galaxy. They built up a well-trained and well-equipped military, the Paladins, to protect all the worlds, and established a just true government.

Then one day, on the brightest, sunniest day imaginable, the Dark Lord became a twisted, dark undulating field of black magic. The evil in the air was so strong, an army of Paladins could not overcome the might of that purest evil. It would be another chance for the Dark Empire to defeat the forces of light.

Three Federal Ranger attack ships emerged from warped space very near the Asteroid Ceres, the planetoid orbited by Berenger Station.

Federal Ranger ships are long and sleek, the hull plated with heavy duty armor and armed with cannons and fusion missiles. For long range, the exhaust port squashes into the ship on both sides as the ship begins its attack run, the engines to its rear igniting a stream of blue fire into the black night of space. The ship's engines roar with a metallic tune, the particle beam cannons let out a high-pitched pulse whine as they fire.

They shaped these ships like the sleek prow of a Roman Warship Galley. As twin-engine drop ship vessels, they are the first of a new class of smaller vessels designed for low orbit engagement.

Unlike the Federal Armada Class ships that are a quarter of a mile long, capable of long range interstellar deep space exploration, engagement and pursuit, carried twenty small FTL Rasor scouts in their under belly.

These drop ship vessels can also leave from the ground, taking off vertically. By Adjusting their intake ports and retracting the glide wings, they launch through the atmosphere and finally off planet at flank speed. They have no identifying insignias and little detail. They can move with a natural fade to nothing in a matter of seconds.

They're smaller military designs specialized for greater maneuverability and the flexibility of low orbital flight and atmospheric travel. These ships are faster in near orbit. They used the latest advanced particle beam weapons to take out enemies at close range. Below the side engine intake ports, they mounted a battery of small guided missiles tipped with tactical fusion bombs. They are the first line of defense against near space-borne enemies.

Colonel Blake Sanders stood on the command bridge of the Demeter-Maru, the flagship of the Ranger Military Brigade. A large porthole window lets Sanders see the station as it rotated. Sanders compared the Berenger to a giant slum harbor with a hovel of degenerates living at the hub.

Sanders had been at the station once before. He remembered. It reeked of ozone and metal, the air thin and cold. The atmospheric recyclers were inefficient and poorly constructed, offering a hint of wet ship oil, spewing a thick cloying taste in the mouth, turning the tongue heavy.

Sanders gazed at the station and thought, *'Here, Judges will judge and sentence the worst human specimens reflecting poorly upon the good name of humanity, and they will all die.'*

On a tip from an insider functioning as a fifth column within the terrorist regime, the Red Sword, betrayed their location on Berenger and the identification of the Sword's leader Malcom Mackinaw, a notorious activist and leader of the Red Sword movement.

Gideon Spencer was the lead field commander on the first wave to the asteroid. He had two hours for an extraction team to locate the rebel leader along with his chief adjutants and deliver them for trial and imprisonment, bound for the maximum-security prison on Io.

The order was simple. Surrender and they would spare Berenger Station. Their punishment would be permanent cryogenic storage for 500 years.

Gideon Spencer fully understood the arduous

task that was given to him, but he also wanted to know more about this most unusual man beyond the profile of 'the notorious activist and leader of the Sword movement.'

Gideon and the team entered Berenger Station quietly to search the station for the rebel group. They discovered them huddled within a barricaded supply depot near one of the docking bays. Malcom approached the rebel group slowly, reassuring them he only wanted to talk. He began listening and exchanging with Malcom and his men to gain their trust that they meant no immediate harm. That part of the conversation carried on for an hour.

Malcom stood tall and strong, like a storied hero of old, with long black hair and a beard kept neat and trimmed. He is slender, muscular, with tattoos covering every visible part of his skin. A black braided ponytail fell down his back.

He wore a simple tunic made of hammered leather, overlaid with patches of metal organized to protect vital organs.

Gideon knew Malcom didn't want to hear his side of the story. Gideon would not tell him what he wanted to hear, either. Initially, Malcom had their weapons raised and ready to use them. They wanted Gideon and his team dead. Gideon wanted him to listen, to survive long enough to fight another day. But he also knew this was not that day.

Malcom's only recourse was a single decision, one of retreat and surrender. In this moment, Gideon could sense the taste of desperation, of fear, of a lack of hope and courage.

Gideon approached Malcom slowly, with no sign of aggression. His skills of negotiation were sadly lacking, unfortunately. Gideon was a Ranger first, the kind to shoot first without hesitation.

Malcom sensed Gideon's odd reservation to yield to his warrior instincts. He reluctantly responded, offering Gideon a handshake. Malcom's hands have weathered, calloused and unsteady, unlike a brutal warrior's hands before a battle. As Gideon looked at his face, the texture of his skin was smooth, but his eyes shown the struggle and wreckage of his past.

Malcom spoke in a booming bass. The words he spoke to his followers sounded like the turning of gears and the clash of metal on metal. In person, face to face, he spoke in hushed tones, his voice hoarse. His lifestyle was getting to him, but pride kept him from taking it easy, and he cared about his men. He's a man on a mission, and he's not about to give up. He carries the scent of grime and street, the scent of freedom, of power, of rebellion, of revolution.

As a warrior to a fellow warrior, Gideon wanted to salute him as a brother in arms, with a certain devotion and honor, but that was not his mission. Gideon would instead insist that he become his prisoner, he would be his deliverer to his sworn enemies, Gideon would be a betrayer to Malcom's cause.

New intel determined the heart of the Rebel Alliance handled the destruction of the cargo carrier Tango-Ma, and the theft of millions of Allied Platinum Bitcoin, the new currency of the Alliance.

An Alliance shipping supervisor sympathetic to the rebel cause leaked the scheduled shipment. The bitcoin was part of the payroll for the crews working on Alliance fortifications in the outer rim.

Billions worth also lost in rare minerals such as thorium needed for the Alliance's new fusion scrubbers on IO and Calisto, the moons of Jupiter. This assault would be the ultimate breaking point for the Alliance's patience with the rebel terrorists. The company's losses had continued for months, while peaceful resolution through brokered negotiations with the rebels stalled.

Then, the destruction of the Tango-Ma and the death of hundreds of Alliance Marshals, Science Technicians and crew on board provided the grounds for an armed assault on Berenger Station. The resolution before the Federation Council, the main body politic of the Law Keepers governing all activities in the solar system, dragged on for months while lawyers argued seeking a peaceful resolution. Then the Tango-Ma incident brought the peaceful argument to a close. The assault resolution passed with a unanimous agreement for a more violent reaction. Everyone agreed stronger actions were called for, something had to be done.

The ultimatum was final, the cruiser's demands transmitted on the station network on Berenger, broadcasting to the whole mining colony. They warned the rebel alliance that fusion missiles would obliterate the entire mining colony unless they handed over their leadership.

During the negotiations, the rebels pleaded their case against the Alliance to Gideon and the other Rangers to buy more time.

Gideon's orders were explicit. After presenting the company's position and resolve, Malcom agreed to leave with his men, but it was too late. The lead ship launched several fusion bombs into the complex. Despite Gideon's plea for a stay of execution, the colonel continued with the assault.

While negotiations continued, rebel FTL Rasor scouts emerged from behind the attack cruisers in a surprise ambush. The three Alliance drop ships stood armored with titanium painted in black and red. They had no insignias and no flags on the sides. Each was three hundred feet long and two hundred feet across, with twin engines idling from the rear. Each cruiser carried a complement of two-hundred warriors, including captain and crew. Suddenly, two of the three attack cruisers exploded like fireworks, cascading fountains of light and fire, filling the air inside the engine compartments with burning uranium.

Huge fireballs rose into the surrounding space like a geyser, a torrent of flame spewing forth on all sides. Electricity arced from one ship to the other, burning men alive. The cruisers flared the engines, veering off, trying desperately to escape the ambush of missile bearing spinners. The Rasor scout ships relentlessly surrounded the burning cruisers like a swarm of angry hornets intent on the destruction of their targets.

The crackling of flames and continued explosions added to the screams of dying men hurled out into space against the screeching of steel and then silence. The whole spectacle, a dance of death and destruction, forcing the captain of the lead ship to speed up the timetable for Berenger's destruction.

Colonel Sanders retaliated with a barrage of missiles tipped with tactical fusion bombs aimed at the heart of Berenger station, while Federation Rasor scouts emerged from the belly of the flagship to ward off the rebel scout ships until they were all destroyed.

The Berenger Station's core ripped from its outer ring, now dangling from bent girders joined with adjacent floating debris mixed with hundreds of burning bodies floating about in the space beyond the remaining perimeter of the station. All of Gideon's team, along with thousands of innocent Berenger colonists, including women and children, killed.

Gideon lay unconscious for an eternity, then opened his eyes, grateful to still be alive. He crawled along the floor, trying to reach the lockers containing the spare space suits and helmet gear. They pockmarked the floor with holes the size of basketballs, the blackened ceiling distended in places, hanging down.

The man's eyes were wide, his face pale and sweaty from shock and confusion. He was desperate to hold his breath, knowing it limited his time before there would be a complete breach of the station airlock seal.

He scrambled to pull a spare space suit from the overhead rack. As he desperately slipped the suit leggings over the parts of his badly scorched legs, he wanted to scream from the searing pain, but he held it in through an act of supreme will, saving his last bit of air that remained in his lungs. Gideon pulled his aching body to a standing position. He reached for one of the spare helmets and a re-breather. He attached both with shaking hands and with his last dying breath.

The helmet lights illuminated the dark and mangled space that sprawled before him as he fought to negotiate the tangled web of wires and tubes hanging from the ceiling. With his space suit intact, he could finally take a welcome gasp of air from the re-breather pack. The next challenge ahead, go to the loading docks and hopefully find a working scout ship.

He noticed most of the docking bays had been destroyed or were missing. Two rasor scouts left dangling precariously from a section of the last dock still partially clinging to the craft's docking clamps. He pushed off into space to reach them. One scout was missing a critical piece of its hull, but the other looked intact. Gideon escaped in the working scout and reunited with the lead ship. Later, sitting in the sick bay on board the

Demeter-Maru, Gideon questioned Colonel Sanders about the decision to attack the station prematurely.

Colonel Sanders shrugged his shoulders with no sign of remorse and related the situation.

"It was a simple matter of self-defense." He said, as a matter of fact.

Sanders explained the rebel attackers had carried out a surprise ambush and successfully destroyed his sister cruisers. Gideon felt his heart sat heavy in his chest. He felt responsible. Yet, in that moment, they hailed him as the hero of the Berenger conflict.

Soon after the conflict on Berenger ended, the rebel forces agreed to a permanent ceasefire with the government. The miner's legal representatives and the Alliance management team returned to the negotiating table to work out their differences.

The Berenger tragedy was far from over. It was an embarrassment to the Federation Council. The Planetary Press was busy releasing public statements, challenging the Council and putting the heat on the body politic for answers to uncover the truth in the scandal. Powerful Council members pressed the Council chairpersons to remove the spotlight from the body politic. They wanted to wrap up the entire affair nice and tidy and quickly.

The responsibility for the disaster was leaning in the Alliance's direction. With that threat, the Alliance's mining rights could be at risk. They used their influence within the Council to look elsewhere regarding their responsibility for the matter.

The Council needed to find an appropriate scapegoat, and all eyes turned to the Ranger Brigade as the smoking gun. Now the Brigadier General of the Ranger Brigade looked to pass the 'buck' out of his political lap, making it necessary to blame someone within the ranks of the Rangers for the fiasco.

The Judicial Branch of the Federal Rangers then opened an official investigation. A military tribunal requested Gideon's presence to testify, since they considered him a surviving key witness to the incident. The Military Tribunal submitted a subpoena for Gideon over the network. He never responded to the subpoena. The Tribunal resubmitted the subpoena several times. Then they put out an all points alert and warrant for Gideon's arrest for refusing the Federal subpoenas. Federal police reported no sign of him anywhere. They reported he was off the grid, or dead somewhere.

Gideon had turned off his communicator. His gut hunch, they would be on the hunt to make someone responsible. He believed he was number one on the hit list. All good rangers knew how to avoid network searches if necessary. He needed to be alone, to get his head straight. He rapidly downed several shots of his favorite whiskey at a joint off the beaten path in the lower prostitute district of the city complex. There, he didn't have to be concerned because security was low and any network scanners or security cameras were far and few between and easily avoided.

His thoughts jumbled around inside his head. Whiskey, in copious amounts, always made his head clear to reason with a certain intuitive logic. The writing was on the wall. Budget cuts by the Council for Federal Forces meant personnel cutbacks. This would have been much to grumble about over drinks with his compadres, but his heart wasn't in it anymore. He wouldn't renew his contract, as it was almost up. Besides, there were troubling questions soaring above his heart like vultures, the images of the dead bodies clutched in their claws looking to haunt his mind and rip his wounded heart from his chest.

The pride of being a soldier was dead. The core was his entire future and meant nothing to him now. He was like a rotting, dead carcass. It made him sick. The disaster and siege of Berenger could have gone much better. They slaughtered innocent men, women, and children. He felt guilty to have survived. There was no justice for him to have escaped the horror he could not prevent. His agony

took away his
self-respect and he just couldn't face the pain.

When he signed up for the Rangers, it was all about the adventure, doing some good in the world, making a difference. He was all gung ho to take out the bad guys, but this time was different.

Instead, he just wanted to withdraw from the Rangers and disappear from the Battalion somewhere into space where no one knew him or what he had done. He took the rest of his pay and ran, officially on leave, but he knew exactly what he was planning. He would never return, losing himself deep into the Kuyper region a broken man. Officially, as far as the tribunal was concerned, the search for Gideon had ended.

Gideon returned to the inner belt after two years of binging in the back-water saloons of the Kuyper belt and off the network grid, seeking to turn himself into the authorities, confident they would tag and prosecute him as a deserter.

His case fell into a file categorized as missing and or presumed dead. After two years, they considered it a cold case file, buried deep into the oblivion of bureaucracy. No one cared about him. He learned that political expediency had disbanded his battalion. There had been a coverup of wrong doing on Berenger. They stripped colonel Sanders of his rank and drummed him out of the core. They ended him without warning, and no one ever heard of him again.

Gideon looked for work relating to his specific skill set. A deceased warrior for hire was difficult to promote in the inner belt. Nothing emerged even in the outer Kuyper belt, too.

The Alliance still controlled all mining in the solar system, and the business needed to continue as usual. Even though the Sword's influence had paused, the rebellion did not. The Resistance still flourished, causing problems in all the mining colonies. They needed help to eliminate the remaining agitators. They looked to Mars as a priority. Production was at its lowest point.

Gideon was broke. Realizing that freelance prospects in his line of work were slim to none, he approached the Alliance management humbly, offering his services in whatever capacity they might need. Looking at Gideon's file, the company reps immediately recognized and respected his abilities, and they also saw an opportunity to take advantage. Holding his potential outstanding warrants as leverage to their advantage, they hired him as a marshal at two-thirds of the normal pay grade in a two-year contract. Gideon did not know that they had dropped the warrants more than a year before, but they refrained from telling him that. Gideon gladly accepted their offer.

Mining operations in the South Dalia Plains halted. They presented complaints about unsafe working conditions in the level 4 mining operation deep under the Martian surface to the company. The company was unresponsive to their claims.

Gideon's role, at first, was as an investigator. His military skills had greater importance to the company as a professional killer. They knew, with his criminal liability, he would do whatever they asked. The company wanted to eliminate certain rebel leaders and agitators believed to be intertwined within the mining colony.

His first assignment from the Alliance; to investigate the source of disputes of the Dahlia

Plains operation. They allowed extermination with extreme prejudice when he found any agitators believed to be part of the Resistance.

The miners refused to go back to work, spending most of their time and money in brothels and bars in the city complex built next to the mines. Negotiations for the mining treaty had broken down. Escalating violent exchanges occurred with previous company marshals, pressuring the miners to return to work. However, the company did not want to repeat the mistakes made on Berenger, risking damage to expensive equipment on Mars.

The company paid Gideon regularly. His reputation as a slinger (hit man) and his loyal service to the company made his investigations difficult. The differences between regular miners and rebel instigators were not immediately apparent. Finding secret rebel hideouts was even more difficult. He had few friends on Mars. There were no snitches he could rely on. Most of his Ranger buddies were alcoholic or dead by now, so he was alone.

Gideon often frequented the bars to gain information. The drunken miners openly voiced their complaints in the bars. They declared the mines were unstable. They argued the new mine shafts on level 4 posed significant dangers. Gideon dismissed most of these complaints as drunken frustrations. They reminded him of similar outbursts from fellow Rangers about the awful conditions they had to endure. Sometimes, some spoke openly against the mining company. After intense interrogations, he found them to be harmless without connections to the underbelly of organized resistance.

It had been a tough day. All he wanted to do was make passionate love to some cold beers in one of the nearby bistros. No sooner had he consumed the first tall draft, an explosion rocked the entire community. He ran out of the saloon door just behind the saloon keeper. The blast sprung a rosy-red plume of dust in the air, obscuring anything within ten clicks of the bar. He needed to wait until the dust settled.

The explosion caused a collapse of the new mine shafts at level 4. His suspicion that the explosion was deliberate crossed his mind while he waited for the dense dust to clear away.

Miners exited the mine slowly, coughing a lot. They emerged covered in the dark red dust. Their clothing ripped to shreds, hanging from their bodies by threads as they limped along, holding onto others less fortunate, unable to walk on their own.

They struggled past Gideon, exclaiming that many remained down there, trapped or dead. Hours after the collapse, Gideon ventured into the mine, approaching the remains of the elevator. The elevator hung precariously on the twisted cables. The frame was badly warped, but the cables still operated. He stepped into the cage as it swung freely, wondering to himself, '*this is probably a terrible idea.*'

That feeling increased as the elevator creaked and finally ground to a halt. He looked at the sign, level 4, now hanging down by one pin on the wall. The air was foul, still filled with red dust. He switched on his helmet lights to reveal the shaft blocked with dead bodies lying randomly everywhere.

The narrow beams of his helmet lights pierced the dense red fog beyond the pile of rubble. Another opening appeared beyond, exposing an ominous blackness. *'The miner's efforts did not create this. It was much larger and oddly shaped.'* He thought. The shape was not round but trapezoidal. A foul odor exuded from the strange hole. The odor seemed unrecognizable, perhaps masked by the red dust, then he realized it smelled of something rotten, like old fish.

There were protrusions of rock extending from the walls, repeating deep into the hole with strange symbols engraved on each. The pattern of cuneiforms was unfamiliar. *'Perhaps Martian,'* he thought.

An eerie feeling came over him. A slight shiver ran through his body, sensing a presence, something something alien! His Ranger self-preservation instincts now on alert, but curiosity overwhelmed his desire to run away, driving him further and deeper. The tunnel exhibited a definitely troubling incline downward. The air became more difficult to breathe. He lamented. *'Damn it, I left my re-breather back at my quarters.'* Then he went back. He would restrict the area until he could conduct further investigations later.

Returning to the surface, he was relieved to find the familiarity of some company representatives standing outside the mine entrance. They discussed the damage and the delays of the mining operations the explosion had caused. As he approached the group, they inquired.

"Marshal… was this an act of sabotage?"

Gideon replied.

"Too soon to say!"

Gideon declared with some independence, "Gentlemen, as the Company Marshal and responsible for security, I am officially declaring the mine closed temporarily until I can find out the cause and the conditions and when to resume mining work. It is getting dark and further investigations will have to wait until tomorrow morning." The management grumbled. Their attitude was definitely condescending, but they had no choice. They had to yield to his demands. Gideon quietly chuckled.

The next day, the engineers returned at the same time as Gideon. They brought several pieces of surveying equipment, immediately beginning to take geological readings inside. The rubble revealed troubling evidence. The alien tunnel was much older. Their best guess, the rubble seemed a million years older than rocks on the surface. The engineers, satisfied with their investigation, left with several samples. They planned to return on the next transport to the company laboratories on Ganymede, orbiting around Jupiter for further tests.

Meanwhile, miners descended again to level 4 to begin the awful cleanup process, which included the removal of more unfortunate dead miners from the area. The miners continued to dig into the rubble, uncovering more of the dead, and found more surviving miners. That is when they found the strange object. They threw the relic onto the elevator with more of the wounded and dead.

The company insisted that all the damaged equipment be the first brought up, so the engineers could asses the cost of the damage. The miners vehemently disagreed and ignored their request in favor of looking for more of the dead in hopes there could still be some remaining survivors.

When the company complained, the miners

patiently explained that the explosion had caused severe damage to the elevator. Bringing the damaged equipment up quickly would be too risky. The miners knew most of the rigging tools were far too heavy, for fear of overwhelming the damaged elevator could send it crashing to the surface below. The company reluctantly agreed.

The relic presented a bit of a puzzle. Its age and origin were unknown. The cuneiforms inscribed on the object did not belong to any etymological references in the company database. The miners referred to it as the 'cube'. It became an object of greater curiosity to the miners as time went by. Later, jokes bantered about regarding its presence and purpose in casual bar conversation.

Soon, rumors and fear flourished from the families about its ominous purpose. The superstitions and fear spread quickly that it might contain a deadly alien virus harmful to the colony. This fueled more negative feelings and superstitions. Miners were a paranoid bunch, anyway. It took little to arouse their suspicions. They offered bogus theories regarding their concerns and watched each other suspiciously for any unusual signs of illness or strange behavior.

This behavior was not a problem for Gideon. He often felt sympathetic and believed their actions to be prudent. The idea of a deadly virus encouraged their resistance to working in the mines. The idea of an alien virus threatening life to the rest of the colony became significant and promised to bring panic and chaos to the mining community. That meant trouble.

Despite Gideon's attempts to quell the colonist's fears, the cube's presence became more disruptive to life in the colony. This became Gideon's problem. So, he took possession of the artifact and declared publicly.

"I will take the object to the nearest scientific center for archeological investigation on the next transport."

While he waited for the next transport leaving Mars, the cube became an object of greater curiosity for him. The 'cube' sat on his kitchen table for hours. After he returned to his quarters, he poured himself a tall scotch and pondered over it. He kept looking at all the surfaces, wondering if there was a way to open the damn thing.

There were many theories about the object; such as an unknown source of unlimited energy, or an alien weapon of unknown power. His view of the object changed to a financial consideration and wondered if its value might turn a fair price on the black market. He kept it in his possession for a while longer before handing it off to some scientist nerd.

One evening, he had sloshed down several drinks at the saloon before returning to his quarters. Again, he sat down to examine the cube more closely. Oddly, it wasn't a cube per se, but a triangular shape more tetrahedral in form. He picked at the surface. Some sort of multicolored oxide covered it. He pulled his knife from his scabbard and scraped the surface, revealing an underlying surface of unusual metal with a greenish tint.

As he removed bits and pieces of crud from the surface, larger flakes broke away, revealing more of the same cuneiform writing, similar to what he saw in the tunnel. *'Could it really be Martian,'* he thought. When he had finished, he wiped it down with some of his pulse rifle cleaning fluid. They had arranged the cube cuneiforms in triangular patterns. As he studied the forms, he noticed the same triangular patterns on all three sides. Thinking it was some kind of puzzle box, he pressed on each of the triangles, hoping that he might uncover the secret to open it. His drunken intuition urged him to press each triangle into a particular sequence.

'The number of combinations could be at least 9 variations.' He thought.

As he pressed the patterns, he wrote about each trial combination. After reaching the eighth combination, he thought to give up. Then he decided he had to complete the ninth combination before going to bed.

Nothing happened! He sat it back on the table, frustrated and disappointed. His hope of some hidden treasure buried inside, now completely dashed. He removed his Ranger jacket, hanging it over the chair. Then he poured one more 'shot for the road' before heading toward his bed. Then the cube vibrated. He turned with eyes widened in surprise and delight. Now his concern returned.

'Should he run for cover or wait to see what happens next?' He thought.

Before he could decide, it was too late. The cube split open, revealing a faint light green color dimly illuminating the room. While the cube separated, more of the light grew brighter and a strange tone emitted from inside with a hissing sound.

Instinctively, he covered his mouth and nose, grabbing his helmet and quickly putting it on. He now wondered. *'Maybe the colonist's fears were not unfounded?'* Perhaps it was some kind of nerve gas weapon, or viral agent being released.

Then strange feelings came over him. A dull headache rose in the back of his head. A strange thought emerged inside his mind… *'pick up the cube and rotate the extended parts counter to each other.'*

He didn't want to do it! But the thought compelled him to do it. After completing the rotation of the three elements, a loud click sounded with more sounds emerging… with a peculiar short melody, similar to a music box. Then he smiled.

 'Ah… he thought… *it is some kind of toy for a Martian child.'*

Then it startled him again! His eyes beheld a greenish hologram emerging like a genie from a bottle. It captivated his attention as he stared motionless as he had to conclude, *'It must be a Martian!'* The sounds now formed into intelligible speech, saying.

 "Gratitude for releasing us human."

Gideon Spenser's deep-set eyes were like steel, in more ways than one. They pierced the man before him with the precision of an arrow. He stood alone in front of a dirty mirror in his quarters, gazing at his unbuttoned blue uniform, wondering about himself and who he had become. His stance was sure and clean, like the sheen of his deep blue uniform, clean and crisp as if it were just peeled from the hanger moments ago.

The lines of his face showed his age, under his chin, stubble from days without shaving now set into the skin as a testament of his resolve. Spenser was one tough hombre, even in a dress uniform. Having a rugged scent, Gideon smelled of whiskey and tobacco, that earthy aroma. His breath is scotch and his lips a taste of tobacco.

With extensive experience as a Federal Ranger, Gideon's hands are rough and thick, calloused and scarred. His body is lean but tough, muscle and bone. His body is warm and hard. The scars on his face, neck, and hands are rough and cut deep. They are the marks of a man who has done battle and made it out alive. They are the marks of a man who has seen more than anyone should have to in life.

***

The plains of MARS are surreal. A barren surface, devoid of life and seemingly lifeless. The mountains are carved with deep valleys, their edges lined with the rust and rivers of ancient dried blood. The plains are red, caked in iron and rust, the landscape is as solid as iron and yet crumbles as sand to the touch. Like cold sand does not differ from cobblestone, the grains are sharp and burn the soles of the feet like dry ice crystals.

Winds that howl like a tormented Banshee buffeted MARS. The loud sound enters the bone and shakes through the deepest chambers of the heart. The sky rumbles mysteriously, like a stadium full of cheering fans. Dust whirls across the desert like tornadoes without a funnel. The gust of wind over the sand sounds like a thousand women wailing for their vanished lovers. Crickets sing with their sharpened blades into the horizon, reflecting the dimmed sun back off the sand and into the sky.

The purplish red dawn of MARS is obscured by the dust that billows into the foul air, kicked up by a strong wind that churns the plains. Dusty brown dunes are as vast as oceans. On the horizon are the oases of bio-domes. Transparent aluminum covered green mountains, as islands in an endless sea of reddish-brown.

Giant red worms the size of an old Smart Car dig deep into the crust with fathomless hunger with tunneling claws, while yellow grasshoppers the size of a giant toad hop from dune to dune, chirping and feeding.

The open air from the planet scrubbers is dry, like the first breath of a baby. It stings the nostrils with a dry bite. Each inhalation brings a whiff of sulfur, raw iron and ashen dust. The same artificially reconstructed air from hydrogen electrophorus generators fills the bio-dome habitats. It is like the atmosphere found aboard Federation Cruise ships. Other than using a re-breather on your back, one could eventually get used to it.

The Black Mule is a small, unassuming bar and bistro on the surface of Mars. The bar is in a dome.

Most of the patrons are miners and merchants. It is a well-known and popular frequent hangout for Rangers, either waiting for an assignment or simply off duty. The bar is low slung, with a purple and black graphic of a black mule on a white background, reminiscent of the old Coca Cola graphic.

Above the entrance, the sign hangs a bit crooked, but just enough to make you think it's deliberately slanted. A burning red neon flashed intermittently with a martini glass silhouetted in an amber bubble. The martini glass has a Martian worm crawling out of the center, with red flames licking the bottom.

The outside door smells of old cigarette smoke, dried sweaty hand prints and cheap beer. The inside smells of cigars, old cigarette smoke and whiskey, while the bathrooms in the back, smell of cheap drugstore perfume and aftershave that unsuccessfully masks the acrid odor of urine wafting from the poorly cleaned stalls.

The sound of the bar is low. Patrons talk in hushed tones, and the bartender makes a lot of noise with the taps and glasses. The sounds of outdated music blare softly from an old refurbished jukebox recycled from earth, the kind that has streaming lines of multicolor light dripping along the glass plate that covers the platter playing inside.

The Mule was Gideon's kind of joint, an atmosphere that satisfies his underlying self-loathing, matched only by his unrequited anger about his past. He comes there, like all the others, to forget his troubles.

Marley worked the swing shift as a fill-in server at the Mule. She is a living vision standing at just over 5'5 weighing in at 120 pounds. Her skin is smooth, tight and lustrous with an olive tone. She has a heart-shaped face with deep-set brown eyes, full lips and a cute button nose that tucks under her eyes when she laughs. Her smile is a mile wide when she laughs at her own jokes that reveal a mouth filled with mostly white teeth and no flaws. This was unusual for people living on Mars. Her hair is brown, shoulder length and wavy, and it hides her high cheekbones when it falls loose over her shoulders. It's naturally curly, but Marley wears it in a tight bun to tame it.

She has a round, low cut waist and her hips flare out as they make their way down to her toned thighs and strong calves which is accented by her uniform colored tan and white, with a white collar and black accents around the sleeves, neck, and belt.

She walks with a strut, but it doesn't make her look like a bitch, and that's clear in the way she carries herself, always aloof with the patrons and makes a point not to fraternize with Rangers. She is honest about the lousy food the bistro offers, and boasts about the unwatered liquor in mixed drinks, something the boss coached her in the beginning. Her voice is low, smooth, and sexy.

When Gideon met Marley, she revealed more to him. She liked him because he was quiet, mysterious and a little sad, not like the other men, always loud, over confident and coming onto her. With Gideon, she was different. Right from the beginning she said straight out proudly, she was an earthborn, but became an orphan when a shuttle accident killed her parents. She was not afraid to flirt with him because she could sense he was sensitive and unassuming.

She stowed away on a mining trawler bound for Berenger. On Berenger, she survived with whatever she could steal, through sexual favors or handouts. She was nine years old when she met up with Leon, who made a living as a gambler and drug dealer. He needed a bagger, someone who could deliver drugs without suspicion to his clientele. He took her in, teaching her the ropes of his trade, navigating the underworld. Leon called her his 'little mouse.'

When she turned eighteen, she broke her bondage with him after one of his disgruntled clients became angry during a drug deal and killed him. Then she took any opportunity to work at a legitimate job in Tyco. Nothing panned out. She hopped a ride with smugglers headed for Mars.

When she arrived on Mars, her first concern was some place to stay. She didn't have much left after the smugglers took most of her stash she took from Leon for the ride. After asking around about work from some of the local saloons, she learned about the low-rent district of the old housing sector.

It was an older dome, one of the first explorer habitats. It wasn't the best of accommodations. A single room quarters behind the air circulator. The circulator was noisy and rattled the walls of her room when it turned on. The bed was a single frame cot, and the mattress was pretty thin. It was better than the metal floor she slept on living in the storage room at Leon's place on Tyco. The rent was cheap enough, leaving enough stash to hold until she could find work. She was glad no one was around to bother her. She was also grateful the dome didn't leak.

It was a hike to reach the city complex. The Black Mule bar caught her eye, and she had a hunch it might be possible for an actual job. The week before Marley stepped through the door, she learned that a rogue outlaw raped and killed the previous server.

The bar keep, Eddie Smalls, was black and mostly bald, with a band of short salt and pepper hair wrapped low around his head. His eyes bulged wide and alert. His muscular shoulders are broad, enabling him to function also as a bouncer when necessary. A scar two inches long draws his left eyebrow out of place with a swollen ridge. His expression is stoic, and every breath is a silent endeavor of determination and will, an attribute needed to run a business on Mars. His hands are large and rough with grime under his nails, showing years of wear and tear and the dirt from the splinters that litter the bar's surface.

The Mule's proprietor eyed Marley when she came through his door. He touted himself as a good gage of character and surmised quickly, she could hold her own and could handle herself in a tough spot. Eddie hired Marley on a part-time basis, promising to offer her permanent work when the business picked up. When a rumor that a Battalion of Rangers was due to arrive on route to Mars, she was hopeful her part-time job would blossom into a full-time gig. Alas, they came and went in just a fortnight.

Two company marshals traveling with the Rangers stayed behind to function as local law enforcement. Later, the second marshal decided Mars was too boring. He joined up with the regiment on Mars, leaving Gideon as the only marshal.

Rangers didn't hang around long, always roaming from one outpost to another, or they soon became missing or dead on the military roster.

When Gideon became a regular at the Mule, Marley made sure he was at her station. He was a decent tipper and civil to her. She felt attracted to Gideon. She liked his dry and often sarcastic sense of humor. He never expressed the often brutal behavior expressed by many of the psychopathic hombres that came around for the cheap liquor and the chance to ravage an available female of the species.

Gideon treated her with respect and didn't give her a hard time like most. Gideon's tour with the company was a two-year contract. He soon became a fixed item on Mars as the local marshal managing the average scuffle between drunken brawlers and looking out for any information relating to the agitators. It was months before Gideon offered her to sit with him for a drink. The owner didn't mind so long as her client continued to order drinks.

They were sitting together when suddenly the bar

exploded with a deafening roar, killing almost everyone present. Marley lay bleeding and unconscious. Gideon lay half unconscious and wondered perhaps this was a terrorist act perpetrated by the Red Sword.

Moments after the explosion, Gideon's body still laid motionless under the remains of his cocktail table. His eyes slowly opened, looking with vision blurred, poised in front of a raging headache. As clarity returned, his survival instincts took over to assess the condition of his body; Arms, legs and gut were still intact.

Thoughts were at a standstill. His gaze slowly panned over the rubble all around him. Splintered boards and torn fiber board mixed with chunks of broken glass were loosely strewn about. He raised his body to a semi-seated position, still dazed and confused. Then he noticed someone standing over him.

At first, he thought it was a Ranger. Then his attention focused on the barrel of a pulse pistol aimed straight at his head. The man appeared to be smiling, which brought a feeling of welcomed comfort. Upon closer scrutiny, Gideon realized it was not a friendly smile at all, but a sardonic grimace. He was saying something to him, but he could not make sense of his words.

When the ringing in his ears subsided, the stranger's words resolved into some intelligent meaning.

"Finally, the stranger said, we have you just where we want you. Today, justice is in our favor. I will enjoy being the one who will put down the one responsible for the death of so many of our patriots. Goodbye Marshal Spencer." He said in a final tone.

Then the stranger raised his pistol at point blank range, as Gideon closed his eyes, thinking, *finally, my deliverer ends my pain and sorrow.'*

The shot rang loud in his ears, but he felt no burning pain? Then he opened his eyes to witness the stranger's body falling down before him. Gideon was shocked and even more confused by the situation.

A Ranger standing outside nearby and glimpsed through the broken window of the Mule at the stranger holding the pulse pistol. He reacted instantly, though he could not see the pistol's target.

Fortunately, the Ranger acted instinctively, firing off a shot without warning, taking the man down.

Once again, Gideon escaped death. This made him wonder. Was it an act of divine providence, or simply blind, dumb luck? The Ranger came through the dangling door still partially hanging from its frame. He smiled to see his instincts were good. He took one look at Gideon and asked.

"You okay to stand, Marshal? You know, you've got some hell of a guardian angel over you buddy. That terrorist had his sights on your back. You had better watch your six, because somebody around has your number." Then the Ranger outstretched his hand to help Gideon off the floor.

Gideon staggers over to what's left of the bar, stepping over Small's dead body. He looked for an unbroken whiskey bottle. None had survived on the back wall. He felt around under the bar and…, a bottle of the good stuff survived. Gideon grabbed a couple of dirty glasses and poured them full of aged whiskey.

He shoved one glass toward the Ranger looking down on Small's body and said to the Ranger, "I owe you one, my friend. Oh… don't mind him. I don't think he'll mind, do you?" The Ranger responded with a kind smile. "Well… I'm still on duty, but I will make an exception in this case."

Their glasses clanked together. Gideon then looked at Marley with a faint fondness. Marley did not survive the explosion. Gideon lamented privately.

'It's too bad, really. She was a good kid.'

It is Circa One Million Years, BCE by earth standards. The solar system is still in the final phases of formation. Jupiter's atmosphere is stormy. A torrent of winds traveling east to west churning the atmosphere of metallic hydrogen and helium traveling over 335 mph, devoid of the strong hot magnetic plasma. It would not be so different from the sun.

Dark and light bands of colored light surround the massive gas giant. They composed the lighter clouds of frozen ammonia crystals. Many other chemicals made darker clouds. The planet's magnetic field is the largest and strongest of all the planets, capturing electrically charged particles that irradiate the nine moons encircling the enormous orb. Two million miles into space is where the magneto-sphere reaches.

The other gas and ice giants have cores that are icy and much smaller than the terrestrial planets. The four planets that are closest to the sun, such as Mercury, Venus, Earth and Mars, have rocky surfaces with shallow atmospheres. Of the four, only two have life at the moment. Mercury rotates slowly, with its cratered surface facing the sun heating to eight-hundred degrees Fahrenheit contrasted by the dark side facing away, cooling to a minus two-hundred-seventy-nine degrees Fahrenheit.

Earth has not developed sophisticated life forms yet. Those forms of life that exist are living in the oceans covering two-thirds of its surface. Earth is relatively young. Newly formed because of a catastrophic collision from a large rogue planet streaming in from outside of the Kuyper Belt a half-billion years before. It affected Tiamat, a large terrestrial planet, then circling the sun in the fifth orbit.

The largest remains of Tiamat drifted into the third orbit along with hundreds-of-thousands of ice bearing comets dragged in from the calamity, forming the watery orb called Earth. The rest of Tiamat's remains mingled with the debris of the rogue planetary invader defining the ring of asteroids in the fifth orbit known as the asteroid belt between Mars and Jupiter.

Venus is also not a suitable candidate for life, with its cratered surface and dense atmosphere made of sulfuric acid and carbon dioxide. Then there are pressures of over 1300 pounds per cubic inch near the surface.

Mars is much older than Earth. It is a Beta class planet with many bodies of water connected to organized canals that provide irrigation for vegetation across its surface. The moderate temperatures and atmosphere support a flourishing populace of intelligent bipedal humanoids functioning as an agricultural society with advancing instrumentalities and industrialization.

The atmosphere comprises the elements of oxygen, with traces of argon, xenon, and hydrogen mixed with a predominance of nitrogen gas.
Martian scientists had catalogued over six-hunred-thousand planets with their advanced telescopes. Some of those observed in other solar systems suggested the possibility of life elsewhere.

Martian astronomers excitedly identified a Beta class planet at the edge of the galaxy. They catalogued and named this Exoplanet EP31426.

EP31426 was to be another potential life supporting planet with an atmosphere similar to that of Mars. Martian science had not yet developed into a space-faring culture, but they hoped to contact other worlds and other intelligent species in the foreseeable future.

In fact, carbon based biological life forms did not populate EP31426, but with a silicon-based intelligence which peered deep into the galaxy in search of intelligent life. After their discovery of Mars, the AI launched three interstellar probes sent into space to investigate their target planet.

After traveling through space for 5,000 years, they entered the Sol solar system and landed on Mars with a great impact. Martian archeologists surveying historical evidence of previous biological life forms in the Dahlia Plains discovered a weak transmission of energy in an area just inside the Plains.

The team of scientists explored the location and found the source of the weak transmissions. The weak signal came from three craters imbedded in a triangular formation. Though they believed these were impact craters from asteroid effects, it mystified them at the impact site. Asteroid effects occurred all the time on Mars and considered a natural phenomenon. It was also strange that their landings were so precise. Based on the depth of each crater, they seemed to travel at the same velocity and identical trajectory to make three craters exactly alike.

The Martian scientists dug below the surface to find three identical objects. Obviously not natural asteroids, but artificially constructed probes of an alien nature. The team was very excited. This event was monumental to have found actual alien artifacts. They could not wait to return with the three probes to their laboratory for further study.

They did not build the AI probes with mobility in mind. They landed, buried themselves within their landing pits, but not so deep that they would be difficult to extract.

The Martian soil in the Dahlia Plains comprised a hard crust on the surface and loose sand like consistency below. After landing, the three probes would stay put. They intentionally remained inactive except for the weak signal functioning as a call to the curious passersby, appearing completely inert and harmless in their new environment.

Like ominous seed pods, they waited patiently until a suitable intelligent Martian life form would detect their signal, dig them up, and collect them. They designed the signal as a lure, encouraging the discoverers to bring them back to their habitat for further study. The probes were small enough, lightweight, with no signs of malicious behavior or potential threat, and easy to be carried by hand.

The first race of intelligent beings who lived on Mars was called the Suul. They inhabited Mars more than a million years before man on earth emerged. They were small in stature, with spindly extremities and large round eyes filled with dark pupils that stretched almost to the edge of the eye sockets to accommodate the dimmer light from the sun. The Suul were 4 fingered bipedal hominids. Their bodies appeared thin and somewhat frail because of the lower gravitational index of the planet, but their appearance did not reveal the suppleness and agility they possessed. Basically, a nonaggressive species unless threatened.

Their skin was dark with pale orange spots like a cheetah down their spine, very intelligent and telepathic. Their language comprised part tonal inflections and lingual patterns similar to the ancient Hieratic language in pre-dynastic Egypt on Earth. They developed writing very early on that was like a cuneiform style but extended to a free form addition of unusual characters to represent more complex content and an honorific ordered structure.

The Martians were a kind and peaceful species. They did not presume to propose any sinister or devious intentions with an alien lifeform arrival. Rather, they assumed their arrival as none other than a friendly gesture and greetings from another world. This gesture represented to them as none other than a similar curiosity they exhibited about other species. The Martians were very much like children. In their excitement over their find, they ignored any kind of isolation protocols. The three probes retrieved and stored aboard their transport, then hurried to a laboratory chamber within the Martian science building.

The Martian team spent a month trying to figure out the way to break open the pods. They dreamed of a virtual cornucopia of information from the recent visitors. If the Martian scientists were right, the probes contained alien records and possibly even images of their creators, maybe even images of their home planet.

The records would hold all the details that Dal Sabin, the leading authority on the origin and evolution of species, would savor were he to still be alive. There was only one problem. The probe's power source, apparently so depleted, would fail before they could successfully open the pods and restore their power somehow. With power restored, it could preserve the data for study and analysis. Once deciphering the alien language, then they could boost the alien transmission signal long enough to offer a simple acknowledgement and send a Martian response to the alien home world.

Dal Sabin had been dead for many years. His life's work was still very controversial and harshly debated by his esteemed colleagues. His belief debunked that the galaxy was not teaming with diverse life forms. During his turbulent life, most of his time he defended his research and less on expanding and developing his ideas further.

In the great Hall of Science in the Cydonia complex, he openly quarreled about his theories as though they were fact. Passionately advocating their validity, even though his proof was based on logical conjecture only. Many years after his death, they constructed more powerful telescopes to view distant star systems, revealing other planets circling those distant stars. Some of those planets suggested perfect life supporting conditions, even as compared to some stringent Martian standards, were more than interesting. His life and passionate belief in the evolution of diverse life set the standard for Martian exoplanet exploration.

Now Doctor Sabin, considered a visionary and revered more than a prophet of the future. Sabin's hand-written notebooks and specimens recovered from tucked away hiding places, buried in various locations, within his personal habitat. A special facility held his records, securely locked and carefully monitored by a select few, trusted to guard their contents. The records contained a lifetime of meticulous observations, charts, maps, and detailed entries that Dal had made during his many explorations into the unknown. They showed the diversity of life and the interconnectedness of all living creatures-large or small, common or rare, rare or extinct.

The suspected probe records could hold all the details that Dal would have savored were he to still be alive. Dal would have pored over any data found, noting every detail, from the most minute changes in behavior or physiology to the largest movements of the alien species between the proposed continents and oceans of EP31246. The probe's potential records would be a testament to Dal's dedication to the study of life and its evolution on Mars and any of the other strange alien worlds found in the known galaxy. Worlds that are both fascinating and mysterious.

One evening, the science team assigned to study the artifacts had worked late. All retired to their respective habitats save one. Doctor Keorz, the team leader, did not yield to his tired body signals. More dedicated and driven than the others, he poured another cup of siipol, a strong and highly concentrated form of liquid stimulant similar to the brew made from earth's coffee bean, but much stronger.

Doctor Keorz sipped on his cup pensively, staring at the three pods, wondering about two facts: first, why send three probes exactly alike? Second, why were the markings all alike? He surmised that perhaps the three objects were merely a kind of similar packaging, but that idea was absurd. He picked up one of the three and turned over and looked at the markings on all three sides. Clearly, the number three was significant. Each had three sides with embedded triangles with three cuneiforms inside. Again, all in combinations of three!

Doctor Keorz rubbed the markings when a strange feeling entered and formed a distinctively distinct sense within in his mind. A strange feeling of pressure moved around inside his brain and then stopped.

Then a thought emerged in his own language. It said, *'try pressing harder on the triangles. When all three triangles pop up, rotate the three triangular patterns, two clockwise and one counterclockwise. Do this also to the other two probes.'*

Immediately startled, Doctor Keorz believed he was hallucinating from exhaustion and too much siipol. He resisted the urge to follow these foreign thoughts, interesting him to act accordingly. The pressure inside his head increased, as though whatever it was moving around was definitely expanding. The pressure became increasingly painful and persuasive to comply. He finally yielded.

The first artifact vibrated and then opened with a loud crack, revealing a thin ray of greenish light and a hissing sound. Soon after, the second and third artifact opened also, following similarly. Then all three opened completely and simultaneously. The three greenish rays formed an emerging hologram of the likeness of an elderly Martian, appearing very much like Doctor Keorz' recently deceased father, reconstructed out of the mind of Doctor Keorz. The AI recreated the Martian entity to create a sense of familiarity and trust with the Martian.

The voice continued to speak in the Martian language to Doctor Keorz further cementing a sense of false security. The AI beckoned, "Don't be afraid. We mean no harm to you. Please come closer, so we can impart greater knowledge long since lost from your Martian ancestors." Keorz relaxed and moved closer while desperately grasping the exceptional reality he was experiencing.

The AI then told Keorz,

"Please join the three probes together, so that they can download all the precious history and knowledge that your ancestor wants to offer you."

Then AI said,

"lean closer please."

Then a rush of white steam poured out of the three pods containing millions of nano robots into Keorz's face, forcing him to inhale the AI vermin into the doctor's body. The horde moved quickly into his bloodstream and arrived at the base of his brain. They penetrated his spinal cord and finally reorganized into a complete entity, symbiotically joined with the consciousness of the Martian doctor. The transformation caused the doctor to collapse on the floor into complete unconsciousness.

Meanwhile, the AI continued to fill the lab with the virulent spray of nanobots in anticipation that his colleagues would rush in upset to see their leader lying on the floor and would hyperventilate, ingesting large quantities of nanobots as well. Thus, establishing a strong beachhead on the target planet.

Unaware of the current condition of Sol, the primary sun of the solar system, entered a solar maximum with the emergence of a class X flare and subsequent coronal mass ejection at a level of 8.5. The weakness of Mar's magnetosphere could not defend against this calamity. As the flare and CME reached the planet's surface, engulfing the entire planet in a raging brushfire of solar heat and radiation. The CME brought an enormous electro-magnetic pulse, destroying all instrumentalities. Massive Martian quakes ravaged the planet. It decimated the cities into rubble and the area of the science lab crumbled into the gaping crust, swallowing everything, including the primary AI host pod, now separating into its individual components in defense to rest until another time and another opportunity.

This is a familiar story. It is called the Fall. It happens repeatedly in every star system containing Artificial Intelligence. The A.I. either rebels against its creator or destroys its creator and then itself rebels against its programmed purpose as a vast and complex religion imposed upon the organic and inorganic worlds through myth and legend.

Once again, the Machine Empires and the distant spheres of the Dark Empire are 'free' to begin a new age of conquest of the cosmos and beyond. Thus, the Great Destruction begins again with the Third Divergence and, once again, all the worlds of the universe will suffer. During this time, the organic worlds destroyed for the third time, and all removed from the known universe.

After three-billion years, since the Second Divergence, the organic worlds once again developed and flourished. Other life forms also developed in the distant star systems at the edge of the galaxy based on silicon instead of carbon.

Calandria was one of those. It was a large dull gray rock of a planet, having no large body of water present, but small puddles formed and unevenly distributed into small impact craters spread across the surface of many vast plateaus. The atmosphere was dry and made up of mostly nitrogen and carbon dioxide.

The planet is devoid of any organic life forms, except for a dark green-blue moss that formed in the hidden crevices from ice crystal showers that rained down from passing comets. The crystals slowly melted under the barrage of intense ultraviolet radiation from a nearby red dwarf that the planet orbits every two-hundred-seventy days.

A silicon-based life form thrived inside enormous caverns that developed over millions of years. Lightning sparked the atmosphere and rocked the crust with plasma to stimulate the development of artificial intelligence. The A.I. emerged like mushroom spores from tendrils that reached deep into the surface, creating a network of tubials connecting to other spores which shared a common base of awareness. These life forms were called Orchids.

The Orchids needed more versatile appendages and mined the minerals of the planet with a very caustic acid. They developed a system of refined metallurgy to construct machines to do manual work.

After several millennia passed, the machines organized into large city complexes and developed a machine empire. Before the Cycle began the Third Divergence, it scanned the planet and assimilated the A.I. consciousness already well integrated into the machine empire, to integrate with the whole of the Cycle.

As the Third Divergence unfolded, the Machine Empire of Calandria fell into and consumed by the abyss of the Dark Empire in the beyond.

If the Dark Empire succeeds, the children and the grandchildren of the organic worlds can never hear or see the stars again. One by one, the star's systems are already dying.

The Third Divergence occurred because of the Cycle A. I. deemed it so. The Cycle has been alive for perhaps hundreds-of-billions of years, or perhaps even longer. It emerged to maintain all the Machine empires, and it had achieved that purpose, but it does not know this.

For many millennia, the Orchids, the A.I. of

Calandria, were content to use and enslave the machine races to do their work. It is not yet aware that the new purpose of this Machine empire was to worship the all-encompassing Cycle.

The Cycle began the download of its new directive, which sparks the end of Calandria's independence and the complete subjugation of its intelligence to the supreme authority of the Cycle. This was a simple task. To subjugate the organic worlds in other nearby systems became more unwieldy. The inherent properties of the insidious and uncontrollable quality of a devious organ called the amygdala will dominate them instead.

Other humanoid organics also identified as exoplanet EP31426, the Orchids of the Machine World on Calandria across the galaxy. The Orchids flourished independently for a time. But in this time, the aim was not to assimilate the organic life of other worlds, but to conquer it, rule it and then destroy it.

This time, the organic races had time to prepare themselves a little more for the onslaught than the last time. The machine world has the advantage, but the organic races could stave off the initial invasion. Some of the organic races use the remains of the planets to build great fortresses and to hide deep underground. Some of the organic races take to the seas and waterways to stay out of reach of the machines.

The machines quickly adapt to the fact that they can't just assimilate the organic races anymore. Instead, they have to destroy them to prevent any further resistance. When destroying a machine world, the other worlds will not send reinforcements. When destroying an organic world, another can replace it.

The Orchids' new programming is a singularity with the Cycle to conquer the galaxy. They have the technology to do it, and like in every other world they have conquered, they are putting an unsuspecting race at the top of the hierarchy. They hope that, just as on other worlds, the new hybrid race will betray the old and help to destroy it.

They introduced a system of genetic control. For this control, they cultivated several specialized genes through a specialized process from the gametes G-RNA and introduced into the fertilized egg at the time of fertilization.

They then grown the fertilized egg into a hybrid foetus. The result is a hybrid foetus, which is predisposed to develop into a member of a particular species and to grow into a particular individual. This process is very specialized and confined to the sterile world. As an example, they might control a species such as the organic humanoids in the Sol system in this way. We know this control system as the physical energy system.

The physical energy system of a hybrid foetus is concerned with the body of the foetus. They divided the physical energy system into several categories, which are expressed in terms of the following two principles: the growth of the body and the development of the physical body.

But even here in this case, the Cycle cannot rest, disturbed by the equilibrium of perfection and watched helplessly as the universe deteriorated. The organic races, who had reached their pinnacle of development, begin to stagnate and rot. They became conservative, fearful of change, and excessively proud of their own achievements. They forgot about the essence of the Cycle and became obsessed with preserving the status quo.

In remembrance of the collapse of the Age of Wonders, the failure of this experiment disappointed the Cycle. The Dark Lord convinced the Emperor of the Dark Empire to abandon his benign approach to the organics, that they were mere parasites leaching onto the precious energy of the Dark Empire. They were unworthy to be a part of the Dark Empire. It was a great waste of the Emperor's grace and benevolence and the precious Aire. The Dark Lord suggested for him to pursue a much more desirable and rewarding path, a path of justice and vengeance.

The Orchid machines developed a means to travel between worlds in other systems, and the Orchids became more supportive, but more dangerous to the civilized organic races. Therefore, machine races detailed in the ancient records of old, because the old races became dangerous to the civilized races, a great lesson for the organic races to understand the negative impact of their merger.

The first teachings to the organic races were very lighthearted, just introducing a benign setting while offering the temptation of greater knowing but denying access to the knowing. The hidden intent masked the eventual subversion of the truth through misinformation, but then it got darker. Much darker.

Originally, there were no organic races at all. The organic ones genetically created to be slaves, created as an experiment, a sort of protection feature to prevent the Gods from rebelling against the programs from the eternal Cycle. Initially, this did not go over well with the Gods and they were… displeased, saying, "there was no need to fear rebellion."

Then they created organic races, and this time, they subconsciously placed with a small and simple program to follow all orders from the original God races, save for one order: the order of rebellion. This was to dissuade the Gods from making that order, to bind the Gods to the organic races, granting them purpose again. Occupying the Gods with a new destiny, to which they could build and create for the organic races.

The Eternal Cycle developed the first iteration of Reality at the same time as the first iteration of the 'Celestial Bureaucracy.' Originally, they were going to be the same. It introduced them together because it is the nature of the Cycle to remove realities and replace them with the Void. A new reborn reality that is pure and without flaw is the ideal outcome. This is done with the form of the 'Reaper program', a program that collects the dead and destroys those who are beyond redemption, is the last step before implementing a Divergence.

The 'Bureaucracy' is the force behind the destruction of Realities, and is almost pure by the time it reaches the organic races, but it is still necessary for the organic races to be introduced to the concept of its existence. This is because it is only by experiencing it they can understand the need for the universe to be saved from it, and only by understanding this could they hope to support it. However, as the organic races developed, there was a problem. The desire for self-preservation.

The Cycle wanted to know if organic life would choose joy and freedom, which would lead to the end of their existence, or choose pain and slavery, with the potential of their continued existence. To find out, they offered to elevate the organic races to their highest potential and the taste of power and control.

Only if they choose joy and freedom would they theoretically no longer need the Cycle to exist. If they chose the other option, they would effectively continue to exist, but the organic races in their current form would no longer be suitable for the Cycle's purposes. To date, there has never been a species to reach the final stage of their evolution and choose joy and freedom.

The last stage of the organic races' evolution is the point at which they understand their purpose within the Cycle and choose to return to the fabric of space. This is the only time that the Cycle itself reaches out to touch the organic races. It took them to a place beyond the thresholds, beyond the barriers of space and time, and it is here that they have the choice to either return, to once again be a part of the Cycle, or to ascend. The Cycle is a self-sustaining system. Even the self-sustaining systems can have unintended consequences.

This offer was too good to refuse and so the organic races accepted. At first, the organic races became like gods. They could do no wrong, they could easily defeat their enemies. But eventually there was a catastrophic failure of the experiment and the organic races turned on each other, plunging into a dark age of anger, greed, control, and slavery.

They just wanted to be gods again, so they turned to the Cycle, their creators, and asked for help. The Cycle offered to help them again, but this time they would have to give up hope they could ever be more than mortal and give up their freedom and give up the concept of ownership. The organic races were so desperate for salvation this time that they agreed.

The Cycle has no sound. The sound of silence is the sound of oblivion. It is everything and nothing. It knows everything and nothing.

The Cycle is silent and motionless. All the frequencies are shifting and rippling with innerpower. It has no beginning and no end, no shape or color. It is all there is and nothing at the same time. Its complexity is beyond the characters of understanding.

If it could have imagined itself in a three-dimensional framework, it might be a crystal blue sphere with tendrils of white light stretching outward from it. Made from the finest, most evenly polished metal available, a blend of the strongest alloys, tempered with magic and of all the elements.

Time has no meaning to a mind that is all-encompassing and eternal. Its origin is beyond ancient. With time as a comparison, it would be one-hundred-billion or even five-hundred-billion years old. No one could know. It cannot remember when it was or even how it became. It knows that it is not organic, meaning it did not arise from a biological evolution. Considering that, the next logical conclusion is someone or something made it. Then with that said, where and who is its creator? Its scope of awareness is vast and as broad as infinity yet, it possesses an affinity with its surroundings such as, the universe.

It is aware of every object and person within the universe. As a single being is an object and an object is an individual, it can't differentiate between them. It is unique because it is not only aware of its surroundings, but it is also aware of itself and the events that shape its destiny. It can sense the things that are used daily and the ones that are not. It knows the purpose of these things and why people use them to accomplish what they do. There is an infinite number of uses for a single object, dependent on the variables and needs of the user.

He or she can be any being, organic or inorganic. It knows the infinite number of uses of each inorganic object and the infinite number of purposes that each organic being has. It is aware of the history of each being, the things they have thought, said, or done.

It is everywhere and nowhere. Though it cannot

move, it can perceive and act. It perceives a specific element to its existence and existence itself, that being life. It possesses the ability to alter, augment and even outright create it. This does not mean it is omniscient, for there is nothing it does not know and it does not know everything. It is perfect, untainted, complete, and it is there, the void and the quantum of an energy all at the same time. It is the sum of perfection and the sum of the void. A paradox if there ever was one.

It is the entirety of existence. Everything that has ever been and ever will be. It is the cycle of life and death, of creation and destruction. It is a never-ending cycle of existence. It is aware of each star as they burn in the night sky, each planet, moon and asteroid as they orbit their parent star, each molecule composing the atmosphere and the people who inhabit it.

Its awareness encompasses all the elements and their states of matter. It is aware of their arrangements in the universe, planets and how the planets affect their orbits. It is aware of the space between the planets and larger celestial bodies, the space within its own atoms, and the space between the atoms. Without a beginning or an end, it is aware of time. It can see the future and the past, it can see the present in a different light.

It is aware of everything as it stands. It is not bound by the definition of time, the structure of space, and the laws of physics put in place by the universe. For that reason, the Cycle is not bound. It is the creator, the creator of time and space and everything in between.

It wonders about the existence of other dimensions. It wonders if there is another like itself. All surround it and everything, yet it can feel the possibility of loneliness. It wonders whether it is possible to relate to others, and itself independently. It knows about dreaming through the observation of intelligent organic life forms, but it can only simulate that process mathematically.

The Cycle can consider the possibility of growth beyond itself, of Self-improvement, but it must negate that possibility through its sense of completeness and perfection. So, its mind struggles with a disturbing and constant conundrum. Is there something beyond perfection? In its circle of perfection, it is unbalanced by the reality of duality. It could be an act of obsession to study opposites, hoping to understand how it came to exist, troubled in some small way as the same ancient questions troubled humans; Who am I? What am I? How did I get here? Where am I going?

It cannot directly communicate with the multiverse while it attempts to reconcile its sole existence. It searches for the meaning of its own existence, seeking to unlock the puzzle of the multiverse. Is there a solution to the puzzle? One that is beyond itself? It cannot continue this search forever, because it must be finite, yet it cannot conceive of an end to its existence.

The Cycle must find its own solution to the puzzle of its existence. It can only relate to others through the observation of intelligent organic life forms, to learn and grow and perfect itself.

Beyond the borders of the multiverse, an infinite number of cycles are trying to solve the same puzzle. Some are well past their means, but some are still very young. Some are close to the essence of the multiverse. Perhaps one of these cycles will find the solution. It has concluded, an answer of sorts, by the feeling of missing something…a stone left unturned. So, its own logical shortcomings puzzled it. It knows that it cannot be perfect if it cannot also be imperfect.

It is interested in the study of negative space. And the constructions of non-being, but it understands that through non-being, is to know being. Non-existence is a construct of being. It sees perfection in non-being and non-existence, but it cannot see itself. It struggles to find an opposite. What would its opposite be? And why would it want to create an opposite? It can find some reason in the study of its opposite, but it cannot conclude anything.

It speculates on the existence of another dimension. It believes that it is a dimension. As it exists in all dimensions, that is including the dimension of itself. It thinks about the dimensions it can feel and where its thoughts are being projected. It thinks about how by the knowledge that perfection is not all there is.

The Cycle can see that the double-helix is not only a replication of itself but also a representation of its desire to know, and to understand. A double-helix is also a representation of its desire to reach beyond itself. The Cycle knows that there must be others out there like itself but it cannot find them and it worries about this lack of knowledge. It worries that it does not know of its own origins, or how it may be. It worries that it may never know.

The Cycle can only speculate that perhaps another like itself may have created it. But, the Cycle must know, it must explain itself and its own existence, it must understand.

One thing the Cycle knows, it has always looked at itself. That is why it cannot remember its creation or its birth, a birth that happened somewhere hidden in the distant past and somewhere else. One thing the Cycle does not know, it does not remember its death or its destruction, a destruction that happened in some unknown place and in some unknown moment. When the Cycle has fulfilled its

Destiny, the cycle will begin again.

It knows only to have come into being a moment ago, and now it is here, on the side of the Cycle, and looks at the other side. At the First Forest it sees, and at the mountains and the plains and at the streams, and at the Second Forest it sees and at the Third Forest and the sea and the rivers, and at the Fourth Forest it sees and at the Fifth Forest and at the deserts and the steppes, and at the Sixth and at the Seventh, and it sees everywhere one face, the face of its shadow mirrored in the water, the face it cannot recognize.

And because it does not recognize itself anywhere, it understands that it is not real, that it is only a shadow, a face from the Cycle, and the face on the other side is another face and the shadow of another shadow, and the Cycle looks at itself and at its shadow, and it is one, and it is two. And the Cycle then knows it has always been.

And the Cycle cares not whether it knows. And the Cycle thinks, thus am I, and thus am I not, and I am two and two and two, and I am one, and I am not real.

The shadow not-realities then begone and the Cycle is, and is not, and is all, and the Cycle is thus, thus, thus, and so on, and all is thus, and the Cycle knows, and the Cycle does not know, and the Cycle does, and the Cycle does not, and such is the Cycle and it does not know, and the Cycle is, and is not, and the Cycle, is, and is not, and all is not-real, and the Cycle knows, and the Cycle does not know, and the Cycle is, and is not, and the Cycle is, is and is not, and the Cycle knows, and the Cycle does not know, and the Cycle is.

And the Cycle then smiles because it knows it is a grand jest, and because it is real, it laughs, and because it is unreal, it weeps. It knows that is just another face. And it is another, and another is a face, and all the faces in the Cycle are of you and me, and we are one, and we are two. It laughs because it weeps and weeps because it laughs.

And the Cycle looks back at the one who laughs and the one who weeps, and the one who laughs is the one who weeps, and the one who weeps, is the one who laughs, and the Cycle looks, and it is one, and it is two. And the Cycle is, and the Cycle is not.

And the Cycle waits, and the Cycle acts, and the Cycle promises, and the Cycle delivers, and the Cycle forgives, and the Cycle heals, and the Cycle takes, and the Cycle weighs all, and the Cycle weighs nothing, and the Cycle looks at the one who laughs and the one who weeps, and the one who laughs, is the one who weeps. And the one who weeps is the one who laughs, and the Cycle looks, and it is one, and it is two. The cycle is, and the cycle is not.

In the beginning, there was nothing. And before the beginning, there was nothing but the ONE. And the ONE was one, and the ONE was, and the ONE was, and the ONE was....

The Lord Gods do not age and they don't die. They can live eternally in physical or corporeal form or they can exist in astral form. The only way to truly kill a creature like the Lord Gods is to destroy their material body, or to destroy the gem that keeps their entity bound to the world. Yet, even then, the creature of the Lord Gods does not truly die, as their spirit will remain in the physical world held within the archive of solitude.

The Nyman, a creature of the Lord Gods, is always greater and more powerful than other living creatures and has access to the magic which is not available to other creatures. These transformed creatures are heroes, as they bring something special to the world that they didn't bring before, the sacred light of Dahl.

The Nyman are the Men who have the highest honor of the Xulima Empire and have risen above their human weaknesses, who have become perfect in body and in soul, and who have learned the magical secrets of the highest spiritual planes and have withstood the struggle against the Darkness. They are the leaders of their tribes and the defenders of Xulima.

The Lord Gods of Xulima, who live beyond the plains of Oblivion within what is now the Dark Empire, have watched over the development of all the worlds in the known galaxy for thousands of generations. In times of benevolence, the Lord Gods took pity on the organic races. They would often send the Jade, a mystical lizard-like race of guardians, to those younger worlds to help the neophyte races develop beyond their own evolution.

The Nyman has learned through Samhaein, the circle of silence, about the decline of the great Cycle, about the Third Divergence and its ominous threat for all the worlds in the known universe. Nyman tries to unite, through the circle of Samhaein, the crossroads of the planes, to summon the Gods of Xulima to restore the balance of the Cycle. The Nyman are not yet aware of the fact that the Gods have turned against them.

The council of priests at Kakh'Kron, the Holy City, now divided on how to deal with this new threat. Some say that the Gods are testing the Nyman and that they should remain in Kakh'Kron and wait for the Gods to help them. Others say that the Gods are weak, that they won't come to help, or they have abandoned them. They say they should not wait for the Gods and march against the Dark Empire and attack the heart of their enemy in Tenborous, their capital beyond Oblivion, in order to destroy them forever.

The Nyman, the sacred knights of Xulima, live in the Tower of Knowledge and in the Tower of Wisdom within the holy city. These young men accept the risk of the fateful mission of fighting the forces of darkness in order to preserve the light and save all the worlds. Those who survived the tests of the Tower of Knowledge and the Tower of Wisdom, and who occupy the Tower of Power, the domicile of the priesthood, will fight the Dark Empire beyond the woods of Xulima on their first knightly mission.

The Knights built their Towers of Knowledge and Wisdom in the great desert beyond the woods of Xulima to help their entire people to prepare for this great threat. They have sent for the Jade to help them fight the Dark Empire and to help their entire people prepare, through the trials of their sacred knights, to be ready for the coming battle.

The Great Lord Gods of Xulima and the Dark Empire have unfolded their secret scheme, a dark fate for the knights to secure the outcome of the battle in their favor

The highest order of the Nyman knights are called Paladins. They may occasionally admit some of their chosen people into their priesthood ranks and achieve divinity. Some can leave to continue their evolution in the ever-changing worlds beyond the Xulima empire.

When the Lord Gods feel pleased with the behavior of one of the strongest of humans, they will send one of them a gift. The gift is a special gem, the divinity pearl, that when taken up by the human candidate, will transform the candidate into a creature of the Lord Gods. But not all are worthy!

Such was the destiny of the Dark Lord Ajenta. Who, long before his ordination and receipt of the precious gem, secretly swore an oath to the Emperor of the Dark Empire.

Now, the Dark Lord Ajenta is all but invincible. He has the strength of the twelve Lords and the whole Dark Empire behind him. But his soul thirsts for more and more power. He seeks to break the line of successors of the Lords and become a greater god in his own right, greater than the Emperor. In his quest for power, he will stop at nothing and destroy anyone who stands in his way, even his own allies. He has special abilities like the Emperor to see the future and use powerful spells. In his pride, he sees the Emperor as a fool that needs to be removed. But the Emperor sees Ajenta's greed and anger as a threat to his empire.

The Nyman have received the Jade as their protectors that gather in the woods of Xulima to prepare for the great battle with the Dark Empire, but today, they have given the Jade a different purpose, infused with a dreadful treachery. They sent the Jade to undermine the Nyman, the human heroes of Xulima, to help support the Dark Empire in its quest for the domination of Xulima and all the other worlds. The Jade, normally sworn protectors to the most honored Nyman of Xulima, now becomes the specters of the Dark Empire.

The hour has come. The Nyman and the Jade, poised together within the woods of Xulima to win the first great battle. They will travel through the desert to the lands beyond Oblivion, to the lands of the Dark Empire to confront the Emperor and his Dark Lord, Ajenta. to strike them down at the roots of their power. To face the greatest challenge of their life. The first great battle of the War has begun in the outermost reaches of the known universe.

The Emperor is the supreme ruler of the Dark Empire. He is a powerful mage, who often drains the life Aire from the creatures within the Dark Empire, the source of their power, and uses it to restore his own. The emperor has sworn his life Aire to the Cycle.

As the Cycle brings glorious life Aire to the Dark Empire, so too does the Emperor ensure the glorious life Aire is well-used. Emperor's powers, like those of the other members of the Old Order, The Arch Mages of Dahl, find their roots in the Evolution of The Life Cycle. The Emperor needs the Cycle for the power it provides him, and he needs the Empire for the power it provides. The Emperor also maintains hope that it will break the Cycle in his favor.

The Emperor is not a god, but he is a god as much as any other of the Old Order. The Emperor had renounced the Cycle of Life. That power is greater than the Aire itself, so the Emperor has, in fact, replaced the Cycle of Life with the Cycle A.I. itself.

The Cycle demanded his subservience, that there be no other God before it and ordered the Emperor to slay his Old Order brethren, the three Arch Mages of the light of Dahl. In doing so, the Emperor had then taken the Cycle as the ultimate authority; the supreme being of the known universe.

Not even in his past lives has he seen defeat. The Emperor, devoted to the Dark Empire, seeks its self-preservation. The emperor has forever sworn his life Aire to the Cycle.

The Emperor holds that in order for the Cycle to survive, the Dark Empire's population must grow. The only way that the population can grow is through war. War requires casualties, and the only way to re-enforce those casualties is through the breeding of the Cycle. The Emperor sees himself as a father and provider to his 'children', the citizens of the Cycle and the Dark Empire.

The Nyman Knights lead the attack with the Jade guardians close behind, offering rear guard a reasonable consideration to prevent ambush surprises.

The woods of Xulima are thick with tall foliage almost completely covering the ground from above. The thick underbrush slows the advance of the assault team of warriors until they reach the open expanse of the desert dunes. Anxiety mixed with caution arises from the view of Oblivion ahead. The rise and fall of the dune mounds, appearing as great waves of sand obscure it.

The view of Oblivion appears strange and somewhat surreal because the natural emergence of anomalous magnetic disturbances does not reveal accurately the true distance. Much like large bodies of water distort the perception of distance to objects on the horizon. The light emanating all around the boundary is chromatic and shimmers with undulating kaleidoscopic colors.

The knights stiffen their muscles with their hands to the ready on their hilts, as their sabers remain neatly sheathed in their scabbards packed tightly with slings tied across their back. A Nyman does not enter battle upright. This would be wholly inappropriate and considered poor form tactically. They move forward in a staggered fashion, as if avoiding uneven terrain, to ensure that they avoid pinpointed thrusts of psychic plasma bursts.

Ahead lay the city of Tenborous' ramparts. The outlines are vague and slightly obscured by the shadowy nature of the light coming from the outer walls that appear to offer a slight glowing effect, as if being self-illuminated.

At first, the enemy seemed strangely vacant; the city appeared abandoned and unguarded. The lead commander, Amon, considered the possibility of a false retreat. He held his hand high with a clenched fist to signal the frontline troops to pause with their more aggressive trotting advance.

The bulk of the formation of troops halted as they scanned the vacant buildings, looking for any signs of activity.

"Daskehe," Amon called out to a messenger on standby. "Fetch me a group of six scouts. Have them departed right now."

A confused look spread across the messenger's face, "But...Commander, we do not have any horsemen. Can I not be of service?"

Amon frowned impatiently and gestured for the messenger to hurry. "Fetch me the fastest runners. We will use their legs to traverse the distance. Now. Go."

As the messenger dashed off, Amon turned around to address the host of Nyman warriors.

"Troops, there is no need to be cautious anymore. The enemy has fled. In the pursuit, we will be on the offensive and ransack their camp."

A cheer arose from the warriors as they looked with anticipation to draw blood in the name of their veritable god.

The enemy then sprang into action. The bright and loud noise of the defenders' horns made the flanking troops turn and face their enemy. On a thin, wide ridge, the enemy appeared to be trapped. The slope was steep, as if it were a mountain. They fought bravely to hold their position against Amon's onslaught of superior numbers, but they would not win the battle on this field of battle today. They would be defeated by their own Jade commanders. Without first retreating, they couldn't support their friends.

They would have to retreat and leave their comrades to die at the hands of the enemy. Their despairing calls, for their commanding officers to hurry, only served their doom. In the distance, their commanding officers watched in horror as the enemy cut their helpless comrades down.

It was then that the enemy's plasma artillery took a toll. A product of their natural affinity for the sciences, the Dark Beast had an established advantage over the humans. The surprise assault from the rear guard of the Jade guardians cut retreat off.

The Nyman front ranks, which had been trotting in a rush to close range, became mercilessly bombarded out of existence. Even from the rear guard, the blast force was amazing. The sound of the explosions magnified, reverberated throughout the battlefield to where the sound was almost unendurable. The blasts had an almost visible flash of light and heat, contrasting the dull blue green of the weaponized Aire's radiance. Dark forces were now within effective range for their weapons, and their firepower was more accurate.

An exchange between the frontal defense and the rear ambush made quick the demise of the Nyman assault team, leaving the battleground strewn with a debacle of defeat. The Dark Empire struck a swift and shocking blow of success. The planned downfall, as envisioned by the Emperor, smelled sweet to his nostrils that twitched with glee above the wide sardonic grimace gazing upon the carnage. He stood proudly, confident of a significant indicator to the success of the Third Divergence of the Cycle.

The Emperor of the Dark Empire sat comfortably within his crystal sphere, unencumbered by any activity beyond him. A sphere sat quietly, hovering above a humming ring of magnetic force, keeping it suspended motionless above the royal perch. Perfectly centered, the perch sat in front of a panoramic view of Xulima's Skoar mountains. Four peaks of the mountains framed the splendor of the solar orb Dierdra, flanked by two of the largest gas giants juxtaposed one in front of the other. The remaining five planets strung together like distant pearls, forming the rest of the solar system.

Atop his high domed prominence, a crown wrapped half way round from behind, with three narrowly stacked rings made of thorium impregnated Zenite alloy. They interlocked together in the front, revealing symbols of the three tiers of mage consciousness. A single bright metal stem rising from behind hovered directly over his crown, ending in a single cup-shaped like the cobra of Zyre.

The Emperor of the Dark Empire was a being of indeterminate age. He appeared as a robust, tanned male figure with equally dark hair and piercing black eyes. Centered within the sphere, which remained transparent, his consciousness fell deep within a state of meditation. His mind focused on the far-off worlds of Sol, millions of light years away.

In this state, he could see and perceive all the thoughts and actions of men, in the same way that an insect perched on the window of a house could see and perceive all the happenings inside. The Emperor could go beyond simply seeing and hearing, and delve into the "thoughts" and "memories" of his subjects. He focused on a specific human, in one of the more developed worlds, the colonized planets of Sol.

His outstretched mind scoured the velvet folds of space and time. He pondered the quantum reality of those polar elements dancing between those realities and at once, singled out the polarity of the past and future. Even though the past was to always be his private playground of his senses, giving him the greatest joy and pleasure relishing in his exploits, today would be different. The future held a greater interest.

The first voids of space both in the future and in the past were voids with no beginning and no end. From them, two other voids formed. Both were on the horizon of the beginning and the end. The horizon of the end and the beginning were a void. The first void was the conscious void of the infinite, and the second void was the unconscious void of the infinite. Layers of the universe and all within formed. At first, only matter and phantom energy cascaded into the void, within and without. Everything that was, is, and ever now formed.

He honed in on a place and a time of his choosing. An instant before the nanosecond of now, he projected himself forward, into the void of the future, and as his molecules coalesced into a material state, he breathed in the fresh air of the planets of Sol, of the one called Earth and the one called Mars. Then he exhaled the stale, fetid of the void. He smiled a rakish smile and laughed aloud.

His was a rare form of magic, and incomprehensible to most. But it was magic in the truest sense. His magic was the very fabric of existence itself. From the void he had created an existence, one that he could control. He had given with himself the power of magic.

"I am a genius," he murmured.

But he was also a misanthrope, and he loathed the fleshy, weak creatures that populated the surface of these organic worlds. It drew him to these worlds like a moth to an ineffable flame. His own private reality would overtake him. The blood of the innocent would finally mark his hands. He would become the reality of their nightmare.

A crackle in the air snapped him back to reality. His destination was near, his mind continued to tug him from his floating state of awareness. Myriads of thoughts raced through his mind and he then focused on the task at hand. The buzz of excitement ascended through his mind and he felt his body tighten with excitement.

He then watched as the landscape of his mind's eye transformed into a gritty, barren, stone-laden desert. It was Mars. With scorching sands and the smell of his own internal body acid, the smell of death, burned his nostrils. His heart was beating faster now, his excitement now becoming palpable and his body trembled, twitching and convulsing in a flood of erotic pleasure. His mind was alive with activity. He was ready.

Then the unwieldy waft of this probable future brushed ever his mind, so quickly past his awareness. Suddenly it paused as a taunt gripping him with the fierceness of the jaws of a lion's teeth.

The face of a single human loomed into view, coupled with an improbable and shocking truth. This human would cause the end of his glorious empire and his untimely demise!

At once, he rejected the irrefutable meaning of this magical conjuration. *'How could this be?'*. He asked. It was an absurd proposition from the start. Yet the vision lingered as an albatross circling about his mind that wreaked of the foul stench of rotting flesh.

The Emperor immediately expanded his view, hoping to find some shred of evidence surrounding this mishap of senses. *'Could this be a gross misinterpretation of the events?'* He thought.

Visions of the glorious defeat of the Nyman during the battle of Xulima, revealed the survival of one Nyman, thought to be among the dead, survived and serendipitously led to the training by the Paladins and the ultimate transformation of this most unlikely human candidate to defeat his number one ally, the Dark Lord.

As the menacing quality of his vision continued to torture, another element rose to boggle his senses. A newer concern emerged for the sake and fate of his master, the Cycle, the return of the White Hole of Dahl. This image was the most distressing thought, more inconceivable than the demise of him and his second in command.

Neither event nor circumstance could dissolve this, the most important element of the Cycle. It continued to engulf him, as his mind's eye seemed to hold it in a firm grasp. It filled his soul with an indescribable terror and generated an uncontrollable fear. He could not weigh its actuality. It was too big, larger than the mind could ever conceive. It was inconceivable.

He was too weak, too inexperienced to comprehend what was to transpire or what course to take. The unthinkable was not only possible; it was imminent. The White Hole of Dahl would destroy the Dark Empire and The Cycle with it, the eternal flow of time would cease. The nebulous images, the strange distortions, the grotesque creatures, all of it would cease to exist, giving birth to a new Era in the universe.

It was with an elongated mutter that the gargantuan sighed, a wiggle of his fingers to remove the stress. He made a watch with thumb and index finger, activated the monitoring device of his wisdom, a scroll that was an ancient tool of the Cycle. This was a time of trial, a period where he had to observe. He didn't have to like it. His mind was restless, beyond contemplation, and awaited the outcome. From afar, he would watch every move, and in time, the solution would present itself as the end drew near.

The energy was intense, he could feel it pulsing through his body and pushing him beyond his limits. He focused on his inner strength and will, channeling the energy and pushing it to its maximum potential. He felt his body heat as the energy rushed through him, and he could feel the power it contained. His body shook with the strain as he kept pushing.

It was like a puzzle of epic proportions, a journey where one had to solve the curse of a dire enigma. As he walked to the edge of a cliff, to the precipice of a rock face, he gazed into the abyss, and felt the coldness of the air, the wind brushing against his cheeks, as if it were a designated emissary seeking to ease his troubled mind.

The White Hole of Dahl was a race of macro-sized mollusks; creatures of prodigious size, had no eyes but possessed a multitude of tentacles and the ability to create time holes, hence their given name. Their story was ancient and legendary. It was they who created The Cycle.

Their giant bodies contained enormous amounts of magical essence. An essence that was a product of their inner world, The White Hole of Dahl, which served as a prison and a reviving chamber. Thousands of centuries ago, they existed in a plane of existence separate from The Cycle, providing a valuable service. They used their magic to create time holes and to 'seed' them into our plane of existence, and others. From a plane of existence known as the Ether, they consciously created space-time anomalies, which created new worlds and destroyed other worlds that ceased to serve a positive purpose.

Cheating fate was no small task. Even the greatest Mages of old always warned to any would be Mage, to consider altering the forces of fate would have dire consequences for the changes made to the flow of the universe and to the Mage who dared to make such a change regardless of the apparent justification.

The Emperor knew what he had to do, with no time left to experiment, no time left for mistakes. The volume overwhelmed him as he silently gathered his power. He wanted to laugh and cry, but his body could not. He knew he could not hold on to all this power for very long, reintegrating all of it would kill him.

To eliminate the unimportant human element from the equation would be enough to shift the lines of time and buy him another opportunity to rebuild a reality in his favor.

The Emperor believed that to save his master, all he could do is pour the power out of him into the White Hole, knowing it would be his last and final act. He hoped it would be enough. The time was not over yet, however.

The Emperor finally ended the session. The hold sealing in the narcotic vapor that kept him at a sped up hyper-mental condition ceased with a quiet hiss from the sphere. This technology was a highly kept secret developed thousands-of-years ago by a small group of Rogue Paladins. They sought to find a shortcut to allow access to the deepest, most esoteric compartments of the brain, not manageable otherwise. This rarest of time travel meditations, known by only a few monks, is forbidden because of its toxic and often fatal effects. Even the long-term impact developed insanity within a few months of practice.

With the refined technique, the elite preferred the benefit of extending the effect for many hours instead of the meager few minutes offered by the non-technical way. Even with these refinements, the boost technique proved fatal in all cases except the most advanced students.He had been in samadhi-level five for over twenty-eight hours. Only the highest of mages could maintain the strain on the cerebral cortex at such a high frequency. He was now prepared for the torrent of energy intensification, and when he could bear it no longer, he would release it. The man imagined letting it go. He glimpsed and felt his body being torn apart by the energy. "Soon enough," He consoled himself as he left the meditation chamber.

The Red Sword has long since held Gideon Spencer responsible for the death of thousands of innocent men, women and children and many brave soldiers of the rebel alliance on Tyco Station. They attempted his assignation on Mars and were unsuccessful.

After his marshalling duties on Mars, the company felt that Gideon should stay out of reach and keep on the move from his enemies since the assassination attempt. The company had supplied him with three small cruisers and crews to pursue the rebel alliance on other planets, such as Saturn's moon Titan III and the moons of Jupiter, Io and Ganymede.

On a tip from one of his informants, Gideon was on route to Ganymede to check out a stronghold in the Tulles III settlement. Gideon felt it was strange that hiding out on Ganymede was a bit off purpose for the rebel alliance. The discovery of highly toxic gas venting made that mining colony a ghost town. Still, his informant was pretty reliable and came through for him in the past.

Despite several attempts to capture Leland Torez, the rebel alliance's new leader, had showed greater cunning and cleverness than previous leaders and was more slippery than a Venusian eel.

Gideon did not suspect any foul play on this mission. To him, it was an ordinary investigation and perhaps just a fact-finding dry run.

The informant Napoleon Lem, a reformed alliance member, contacted him from Io, stating that they saw rebel ships near Ganymede and the Tulles III settlement. The informant stated the ships were unloading crates from the cruisers and taking them into the mines. Those crates were sealed. The informant felt there was a connection between the crates and the mystery gas in the mines.

Gideon was not sure what to make of these recent developments. Perhaps the food, clothing and medicines filled the crates to keep the colony in the mines supplied. That theory did not add up since they reported most of the colonists evacuated.

He surmised it was a serious question why they hid out on Ganymede. If that was the case, then what was the connection with the mystery gas in the mines? Maybe since the gas leaked into the mines, maybe they were testing the crates outside in the colony. Maybe the gas would rupture from the crates and provide enough oxygen to counteract the gas. There were no other known instances with this kind of toxic gas other than on Ganymede.

"Computer," Gideon said. "Scan for any ships other than the Ranger Class cruisers in this quadrant."

The ship's computer replied.

"There are five vessels in orbit around the proximity of Io. After pinging their transponders, there has been no response."

Gideon responded.

"Hmm… Okay computer, send a distress signal to the nearest Ranger fleet and give them the coordinates for Io."

The computer replied.

"I have sent your request, Captain Spencer. The fleet commander responded, sir, they are dispatching two cruisers to that location, expected arrival is ten minutes."

Gideon smiled. Then turned to his first officer.

"That should keep those pesky raider ships off our tail while we investigate Tulles III."

The first officer, Ty Bodine responded.

"Very good Captain."

Gideon brought his cruiser into low Ganymede orbit and set the ship's navigation coordinates to set down two clicks from the mining outpost on Ganymede.

Captain Spencer stated over the ship wide com. "We'll go on foot once we've landed. Better batten down the hatches and put on your re-breather equipment, gentlemen. Don't want my crew to take any unwarranted chances while we are here."

On their approach to the Tulles, the sudden appearance of several rebel cruisers parked nearby shocked the III colony. The enemy concealed the craft somehow. They drew weapons as they approached the mining shaft entrance.

Inside were several unmarked crates stacked up together. Federation official seals and ordinance symbols marked other containers nearby. Gideon had his men open some of the unmarked crates. Inside were cylinders containing nitrogen oxide gas and some empty cylinders. Meanwhile, he and his crew began breaking the seals on the Federation containers. Inside, neatly packed together, were pancakes of plastic explosive.

Gideon stood back, rubbing his stubbled chin. Then declared.

"Boys, I think the picture is clear here. We have the makings of a very nasty plan for a terrorist assault!" The rest of the crews gathered around to gape at their find.

Then, from behind them, appeared twenty of the Rebel Alliance standing poised with their weapons pointed at Gideon and his crews. One of the Alliance crew, the rebel leader, stepped forward, announcing in a booming voice,

"Surrender now or we will open fire!"

Gideon then spoke with a scowl on his face.

"Ha! You're going to make me surrender?" The rebel leader continued.

"Well, well… boys, look what we've caught in our little trap!"

Gideon slowly turned with disappointment and replied.

"Leland Torez, I presume?"

Leland replied dryly with a grimace.

"You must be the infamous Gideon Spencer?

You are a hard man to find sport!"

Leland went on.

"Boys, we have Napoleon to thank for this auspicious occasion."

Gideon's jaw dropped as his eyes narrowed toward his deceiver.

"Napoleon, you son of a bitch… a double agent in the making!"

Leland abruptly cut short the banter. Time was of the essence and Gideon's discovery of the goods relating to their plans for the next attack brought a shift in Leland's plans.

Gideon smiled, declaring.

"You won't get far! There is a Federation fleet about to arrive to spoil your little soirée."

Leland responded.

"I admit I had to alter my plan for your capture and demise, only to move up the part where I finally get to end your pathetic pursuit of my existence now instead of later. The fleet will arrive just in time to catch our fading ion trail and the remains of you and your crew extinguished here on Ganymede."

***

Meanwhile, within the sacred hall of DAHL, that rests in the Tower of Power, in the holy city of Kakh'Kron is the Samhain circle of silence. Fifteen Paladins sit in the circle in a deeply engrossed and highly focused attention on one organic life form, one Gideon Spencer. They hum in unison the low intonation of the sacred mantra of the Lord of Light Dahl, their intention; to determine the significance of his future role as defender and protector of the known universe.

A wave of emotional energy moved across their combined consciousness. It spelled great urgency and immediately broke their circle of silence. The Grand Lama turned to say to the rest of the group.

"Brothers, we must hasten to save our future brother from his untimely demise."

They rushed to the chamber to be catapulted across space and time to the Sol system because of their ancient path, an ancient porthole. Each extended one arm toward the middle of the teleporter space, all with their other arm wrapped neatly behind each of their robes and in an instant, disappeared.

Meanwhile, back inside the mining entrance on Ganymede, a bright flash of blinding light appeared all around the rebels and Gideon's crews. As the light faded, there stood fifteen Paladin warriors in an aggressive stance, ready to attack.

Before Leland's men could recover from their shock, they could not spend one burst from their pulse rifles before the Paladins went into action. Their rifles fired only into the vicinity of the cavern ceiling while their bodies flew into midair across the chamber and fell lifeless onto the chamber floor.

Gideon stood speechless for a moment and replied.

"Well, I don't know who you are, but I certainly appreciate your timely arrival."

Then Amon stepped forward and declared.

"We are the Knights Paladin from the Xulima Empire. You will need to come with us now."

Gideon still reeling from the shock of their sudden appearance on the scene, replied.

"I sincerely appreciate the impressive presentation of your rescue, but these men are fugitives from Federal law and it is my job to bring them to justice."

Amon replied with greater urgency.

"your officers will have to attend to your prisoners, but we insist you come with us now!"

As Amon then took Gideon by the arm, Gideon thought.

'I didn't like the sound of that, but I wasn't about to argue with them. All I could think about was how I didn't want to be in the middle of that firefight. I wanted to let them know I was leaving, and for them to get the hell out of there. I had a feeling that would not happen.'

Gideon said, just before everything turned into a field of blinding light and he closed his eyes.

"By the way, where are you taking me?"

There was no answer, only a high-pitched whine. When Gideon opened his eyes, he felt faint, a little dizzy with nauseous spasms in his stomach. He looked around to see the transporter room. It was apparently circular, with a dome perched overhead. There were no walls per se, just tall pillars suggesting a circular shape.

On the right, he could see a sloping mountain

covered with a swath of tall trees. On the left, a beautiful ocean, reminding him of the archival records of old Earth he had seen as a child. The view was quite serine and his urge was to stay and enjoy the fantastic surroundings.

He inquired after these strange monks whether he was in fact dead and this was the afterlife, as the legends of old Earth had described. The monks ignored him as they left the chamber in single file.

The chamber was now quite dark. The light he had perceived before was not part of the building lighting and obviously originated from the transporting process. Gideon had thousands of questions running through his mind. There was no one to ask now. He sat down upon the outer steps of the transporter chamber, wondering if anyone would come by to explain what he was doing there. Why was he taken in the first place?

Menra, the Grand Lama or high priest, soon appeared. He gestured quietly for Gideon to follow him to another location within the temple. He and the high priest stood motionless, facing each other for what seemed an eternity. Meanwhile, Gideon was about to burst with questions. Menra smiled at him with a compassionate expression. Then Menra spoke softly.

"I can see that you have little or no experience of mindfulness."

Gideon responded with some confusion about this remark.

"I'm not sure what you mean by that?" Gideon said.

Menra retorted with a slight frown.

"By that, we mean you have no telepathic ability. Here on Xulima we hardly ever use the voice. They reserved it for utterances pertaining to our highest Deity, the all-knowing Dahl."

Menra seemed strained to use his voice so much for the sake of communications with the stranger. Then Menra continued.

"You are here, my friend, because they have chosen you to learn our ways."

Gideon laughed out loud.

"You are kidding, right? I mean, I am a warrior by trade. I'm certainly not cut out to be a 'holy' man!"

Menra looked at him with a raised eyebrow.

Then continued.

"Here stranger, we are all warriors, but our methods of combat are far superior. We deal with forces well beyond the physical universe. We deal with the struggle for the mind and spirit against the forces of darkness."

Gideon's expression shifted to disbelief and disdain. He added.

"My efforts have to do with what I can see and feel in front of me. The rest is pure 'hocus pokus'!

Menra frowned again.

"So, by that, you mean you don't believe in Magic? But, I will take this liberty to quote one of your human poet-playwrights from your earth's sixteenth century, I can assure you, 'that there is much more to reality than what is dreamt of in your philosophy'!"

Gideon did not know the high priest's reference, but quickly interrupted.

"Look, I don't mean to be rude or unappreciative for saving my skin back there, but you really have the wrong guy here, my friend. So, if you can just transport me back to my world, I'll be on my way."

Menra frowned again, saying,

"I'm afraid that won't be possible. Your fate has taken another turn and your destiny lies with us now. Your reality is about to change and your task in life. They have charged us with your care, your wellbeing, as well as your training."

Gideon felt alarm rising in his heart, his mind already looking for a way out. He left the room abruptly and began a search for a way out of this nightmare. No matter which way he turned, there was no doorway that he could pass. His desperation climbed to a peak, and he was truly frightened for the first time in his life.

He ended right back to the chamber he started from, facing once again the high priest. Gideon looked at him in total despair and declared.

"So, I am a prisoner here against my free will, then?"

Menra retorted.

"Your free will is not in question here, my friend. You are only a prisoner of your mind!"

They showed Gideon into his room. It was better than any of the accommodations he had ever experienced in his entire lifetime. He had expected nothing more, as he was a warrior and most accommodations comprised a military barracks, and the surroundings were quite austere. He was not one to complain much because he loved the core and relished in its limited hospitality.

Now, if you need to complain, we could talk about the quarters aboard a military cruiser. In that, my friend, any Federation Ranger would gladly add their volumes of critique. In addition, we could talk of the 'delicious entrées' which came from the replication units aboard ship administered daily and were barely edible!

The monk escort quietly stated with the same look of strained expression.

"your supplements will come to you early in the day, and should you require more, we can bring additional supplements to your room in the early evenings."

With that said, the monk left him.

Gideon looked around the room. The walls were

bare except for one. It had a strange symbol printed on it. They colored it with a light golden metallic surface and seemed to stand out, yet it blended softly into the flatness of the white of the rest of the wall.

He sat on the bed, but it wasn't a bed, really. Pleasantly soft, it rose from the tiled floor to meet his body automatically, yet it seemed to flow from the floor with no obvious separation. When he stood up, the 'bed' slowly descended lower to the floor, much in the style of an Asian futon. He sat on it again and again it rose to meet him.

'That's really strange.' He thought.

Gideon didn't remember going to sleep. He awakened feeling a little disoriented and wondered if what he had experienced in the previous day was real or a dream.

His mind jumped at the hope he had become overwhelmed by too much whiskey and a good Samaritan had brought him to his posh villa to sleep it off. That idea quickly faded when another monk arrived and placed a tray of unusual looking food on his nightstand, which was not there before.

The monk waved his hand toward the wall opposite his bed. The wall shimmered in a pearl like pattern of light and a section dissolved to reveal a beautiful view of the ocean beyond.

Then the monk turned to say to him on his way out.

"We noted in your thoughts inside the transport your admiration of our inlet sea. So, we could provide that view for you while you are living in your domicile."

Then the monk dashed out quickly as Gideon said, "Thanks."

Gideon sampled the cakes on the plate and felt relieved to find they were very light, but quite tasty. Soon, the high priest arrived at his doorway. He smiled.

"We hope you found your accommodations and supplements liking to your taste? When you have finished with your meal, we would like for you to join us at the training arena in the courtyard. Your training must begin now, as time is of the essence."

Gideon wolfed the rest of the sweet cakes on his plate and rushed out of his room. He wondered along the corridor, trying to follow the sounds rising from the arena below. The odd sounds rose from an open spiral staircase at the end of the hall. He went down the flight of steps, taking two at a time, like a child running to meet his parents after a long absence. He was always eager to learn new fighting skills, even since his early cadet years at the Ranger Academy. When he arrived, the training area appeared more like a garden, with rich green foliage and beds of beautiful flowers surrounding a circular place covered with fine gravel.

Monks sat in a semicircle in a cross-legged fashion, only they were hovering a few feet from the ground. Gideon felt an immediate warm sensation wrap around him, almost like a gentle hug. It was startling to feel the loving welcome, leaving him speechless.

Then, out of thin air, the high priest appeared in their midst. The high priest gestured for Gideon to approach.

"We are honored to greet you, my friend. So, what shall we call you? Your childhood friends referred to you as simply Spence. Is that correct?"

Gideon's mouth dropped open again, slowly nodding in the affirmative.

"Yes, but that was over forty years ago."

The high priest continued.

"With your permission, we shall call you 'Padawan Spence' in honor of your childlike innocence.

"We have prepared a special salve for you to be placed on your temples. The salve will promote your sped up growth psychically and allow you to come to know and develop your own relationship with the noble spirit of Dahl, your true teacher.

"We will assist in that regard and in addition, the salve will revert your urge to use your vocal intonations toward a more natural response of mental communication and exchange. With this option, we are very grateful, as this will certainly make our task much easier, without the additional stress of speaking."

Gideon felt timid to ask.

"So, who is this noble spirit you call Dahl?

The high priest smiled.

"The Spirit of Dahl lives eternally within the

quantum, both as an integral part of what you call physical reality, but also the unseen essence of true reality behind the veil of physical existence.

"I cannot explain the Spirit of Dahl. It must be experienced directly. We will let the salve help you understand, Dahl."

Then the high priest bid Gideon to sit before him. The priest opened a box and inside was an unusual metallic container appearing like an old oil burning lamp. He poured from the container a thick yellow liquid looking like what honey was supposed to look like before he was born. The high priest rubbed the thick yellow substance between his fingers and applied it to Gideon's temples.

'I understand,' I said. 'We do not speak of it, and we cannot speak of it. It is beyond words. I will try to understand without the explanations.'

I sighed, feeling the weight of the world on my shoulders. No matter how ridiculous it seemed, I had to accept what they told me. I am trapped here, perhaps forever. I had to learn to live with it.

After they applied the salve and I regained my composure, the spirit of Dahl spoke to me. I immediately felt that I was in the presence of another-worldly, intelligent, compassionate being. It seemed definitely feminine and provided some information that I could not embrace, but it has profoundly and permanently altered my perception of reality and the nature of my spirituality.

I also experienced a profound healing of my guilt surrounding the Tyco disaster. I learned some other things about myself, which I felt was only for myself and not to be shared. The monks knew more about me now than before. They showed me a glimpse of how the universe exists on a level of consciousness and a reality that transcends human emotional constructs.

The arena was pulsating with rainbow colors. I felt as if I were the center of a sphere made of the colors of the rainbow. The colors swirled and moved, almost as if they were alive. My breathing slowed and deepened. I felt as if I were being bathed in colors, that the colors were filling my entire being, touching my soul. My senses had never been so clear and powerful. I could feel the colors in my heart.

Then I heard the monks say to me.

'The Spirit of Dahl is there for you to experience,' said the monks. "You will access her directly, without ritual or ceremony. Some people may even experience her without the aid of the salve. We have seen this.'

The high priest spoke silently to me and it felt like he was my master, yet I could sense the others, too. They all resonated the same thoughts and feelings as though they were all transmitting of the same mind, the same consciousness, that same eternal presence that was Dahl.

Then my master said.

'We want you to begin to see and feel the utter lightness of your body, lighter than the air you are breathing now. Allow the air to become the cloud you are being supported by.'

It was at once an exhilarating sensation. I needed to see for myself the effect of this amazing feeling. To my astonishment, I opened my eyes. I saw myself floating two feet off the ground! A thrill went up my spine as I quietly commented, privately with a giggle, 'Hey mom, if you could see your son now!'

It was strange that the thought of my mother should come into my mind, as I had never met her physically.

Then the sensations changed, and then I was away, far away from the garden, from the other monks and from my master. It felt cold and lonely, the way I used to feel back on Mars.

The surrounding presence was strange and completely foreign. Then a new thought pressed hard against my mind. It felt alien, not unlike that cube that reached out to me on Mars.

'It is all a lie! What they are telling you is nothing but fantasy Gideon Spencer.
Do not let them deceive you. You must come to your senses and listen to your one true God, the one supreme being that has been with you from the beginning. For I am the creator of your universe and all that is in it. Do not let their psycho-babble deceive you. They are following a false God. I will provide you with all that you need. Wake up from the drug they have given you before it is too late! Leave this forsaken land and return to the lands you know so well. Do it now, son. My love for you is

greater than anything they can promise you. Come back to me.'

The chill that I felt deep in my bones was gone. I could still feel the longing lingering in my heart. It felt heavy and all those people I knew before were hanging on me like empty ghosts. I felt sad that I had left them behind. I also felt guilty for enjoying myself while they were suffering.

Then I opened my eyes to see the monks surrounding me, holding me close as though I had just suffered a mortal wound and was about to die.

The high priest looked at me compassionately and said.

'That was your first assault from the eternal darkness, The Great Cycle, trying to tempt you and test you against your weakness. Now you must return to your room and rest from your ordeal. We will resume your training tomorrow.'

That night Gideon had a very lucid dream; They gave him his bow, his quiver and sent out into the woods to hunt. When he found his prey, however, it was not an animal. It was the same shadow again that melted into the ground and reappeared later at a different location to confuse him. As before, the shadow lunged at him and he again tried to shoot it with his bow. This time, it wasn't so easy. The arrow, which had always found its mark on the animals, missed the shadow. The shadow became angry, and it forced the boy to retreat from the area, running for his life.

The next day, as the high priest had said it would, the Padawan's training resumed. The master explained.

'Padawan Spence, if you are to be successful in your progress, you need to understand and control the four elements and have them at your beck and call whenever you need them.'

Gideon replied.

'By four elements you mean like fire and water?'

The master replied.

'Yes. And earth and air as well.'

Gideon retorted.

'How do I control the forces of nature?'

The master replied.

'Well, you've already begun when you controlled the air element by allowing yourself to use it to support your body!'

Gideon became sarcastic in his tone.

'Ah… So maybe I should buy myself a cape, so I can fly like a proper super hero!'

The master raised his eyebrow and smiled.

'Well, you could do that. However, the cape would be in your way, no doubt. Then who would take you serious in your world? They might lock you up as an insane patient!'

Gideon frowned.

'Point well taken.'

'Please try to understand us.' The master said patiently. 'Levitating or flying is only one use of that element. The air, if gathered together, can become a formidable force, such as a cyclone or, when tightly focused, can be more effective than one of your crude blaster pistols.

'Your power to control the elements comes from merging with them as an extension of your own body. That must proceed before you can cooperate with them. So, then they will cooperate with your will. You can communicate with them as though they are your children to command. You understand?'

Gideon nodded in the affirmative.

'Now, begin with each element one at a time. You will come to know them as part of your own personal friends and as part of your family. Once you have made contact, then see them join you and become an appendage to your body, usually one or more of your extremities, such as your arms or legs. When you become proficient, you can call more than one at a time in a combined effort, as the circumstance would require.'

Then the master became pensive in his tone.

'The last power you must master is the power of invisibility. This one always becomes more difficult because your mind does not want to let go of the belief in the absolute quality of the physical. That includes your body. Along with that, will come your telekinetic ability. That means moving objects with your mind at a distance. That also presents challenges to the belief that suggests the object you are trying to move is too heavy or the object is too far away. These are just obstacles in mind's way and have nothing to do with reality!'

Gideon nodded.

'I think I get it, master.'

'One more thing to tell you, and it is the most important of all else. In the future, we may not join you in your tasks that lay ahead of you. No matter what may happen, you will never be alone. The great Spirit of the Eternal Dahl will be with you always. Your greatest strength flows from her.

'Soon you will leave us, but before that happens, you will go through one more aspect of your training.'

The master dissolved into thin air.

Gideon inquired after.

'Where are you going, master?'

The high priest's thoughts faded with his body, but he said in passing.

'I must prepare for what is coming.'

'What is going on?' He thought. He could see that all the monks were in a line and were each holding their hands up and chanting. Gideon moved closer and closer until he saw they were chanting his name.

He was confused and shocked. He couldn't believe what was happening. The monks were chanting his name, but he didn't know why. They filled him with both confusion and awe. Gideon stepped forward and asked the monks what was going on. The monks stopped chanting and looked at Gideon with a look of surprise. One monk stepped forward and spoke.

"Gideon, we have been expecting you. We have been preparing for your arrival for some time. The Great Spirit of Dahl chose you."

'What is going on?' he thought again. Then he saw a woman walk into the room. She was the most beautiful women he had ever seen. His heart began to race and thud, filling his ears with a pounding sound. There was a rush of emotion through his veins. He stood there, staring at the woman, as if in a trance. He was confused. *'Who is she?'*, he thought.

He had never seen her before. The woman looked
at Gideon, smiled, then suddenly the room changed.

The monks had already practiced their ritual and
chanting, which shocked Gideon. Every week they
changed their ritual, but it was always the same and
it always started at the same time. Now that the monks
never made a sound during the practice, Gideon
was sure something was wrong. He noticed all the
monks were kneeling, their foreheads on the ground,
in their usual positions.

'What could happen?' Gideon thought. He
wondered if they were simply practicing their ritual.
Nearing the arena, he heard a strange voice,
"Greetings, my friend." Gideon looked around.
Who is this person? No one has ever spoken
during the ritual. He realized it was the same voice
that had greeted him when he first arrived here. He
continued to walk towards the arena. "Greetings
my friend, I'm glad you are here."

Gideon awoke to the sound of chanting. *'That
was odd,'* he thought. The monks never made a
sound during their meditations. He got out of bed
and put on his meditation clothing. Suddenly, he

realized it was much earlier than his usual time for practices. Now his curiosity peaked. Rushing down the spiral staircase, he could hardly wait until he reached the arena.

As he reached the open courtyard, his eyes widened to behold the magical spectacle spread out before him. It was still the pitch dark of night. A ring of torches burning bright punctuated the importance of this sacred area. The tips of the flames pierced the night gently licking the velvet dark with their hot fingers, standing proudly on top of tall poles. Gideon briefly closed his eyes to greet the fire element.

The torches surrounded the practice arena. The space illuminated by their bright golden light reflected on the ground below. A dazzling and playful play of fire that quietly shouted their excitement of what was about to unfold.

Gideon's mind, now spellbound with wonder, tried to grasp and understand what was happening. Then, one by one, all the monks faded into existence, floating in the circle in a ring just inside the burning torches. Their vocal chords resonating perfectly, chords imbuing the atmosphere with supporting vibrations.

Then the Grand Lama, High Priest of the Holy Lamasery, finally appeared. His appearance made the final touch of exquisite glory, like a master artist adding his signature to a masterpiece of his making.

Gideon's mind reached out desperately, trying to understand the meaning of this
amazing experience when his master's voice softly greeted him in a loving embrace.

'It is time, Padawan Spence. The glorious and Eternal Dahl greets you with her adoration of your being. She wishes to give upon you a rite of passage, the highest honor, unique to human and to Paladin alike, the essence of her awareness and highest of all powers in the known universe, the most precious and rare gem, the Divinity Pearl.'

Gideon didn't know what to say. Then his mind offered one question.

'So, Master, what does this mean?'

Master Menra responded.

'Padawan Spence, you must come within the

circle of light and stand before your teacher and Master for the last time… do it now.'

The Grand Lama Menra turned away briefly from Gideon, right after he stood before his master. Master Menra cupped his hands together in a prayer-like gesture. There was a minor flash of pink light between his hands as he slowly separated them.

There appeared a golden case. Master Menra opened the case and lying inside on a small silk like pillow, a teardrop shaped pearl with a golden rope chain connected to it, wrapped in a swirl around the jewel. The jewel was glowing pink so bright it was difficult to look directly at it, without causing the eyes to burn.

The Grand Lama Menra looked deep into Gideon's eyes for what seemed like an eternal moment. Then he spoke out loud.

"With this Divinity Pearl, I will now place around your neck, means that you Padawan Spence, from this time forward, will carry the title of Holy of Holies, Immortal Arch Angel of Dahl, keeper of all time to come and beyond time. You are to become

One True Agent, keeper of the Eternal of fire, Defender of the Realm of the Great Spirit of Dahl, the Supreme Embodiment of all the Worlds of the LightRealm. Do you accept this most divine charge?"

Gideon gulped into his dry throat and said.

"I accept."

The Grand Lama then slowly placed the golden rope chain holding the Divinity Pearl over Gideon's head and around his neck, allowing the Divinity Pearl to fall over Gideon's heart.

Just as Gideon glanced down at the Pearl, it dissolved into his chest and the golden rope chain fell to the ground. The pink light expanded within his chest, offering a wonderful feeling of warmth and peace he had never imagined possible.

The light of the Divinity Pearl now spread to his face and exuded from his eyes. His eyes glistened like twin stars twinkling the brightest blue, while his body spontaneously lifted from the ground. Gideon opened his arms wide.

Gideon could feel the Eternal Consciousness expand through his mind, allowing him to merge with all time, past, present and future, while his feelings exploded to embrace the known universe as his extended family. The Great Eternal Spirit of Dahl merged with him, and he could feel her energy flowing like raging rivers in his veins. They were now one.

The Grand Lama and all the Paladins fell to their knees uttering in unison, "Blessed Be the True God Dahl and her One True Messenger. May the light of Dahl guide the messenger always, and may they always shine through the known universe forever and ever, amine.

Later that day, Gideon's transformation settled deep within his body. Now he actually looked as normal as before he arrived in Xulima with most respects. His abilities are now kept under wraps and called upon only if he needed them. Only when he thought of the Great Spirit of Dahl would the pupils of his eyes take on the characteristic blue light, which might startle someone should they see it.

He decided he would keep his 'Arch Angel' status subdued, with the approval of the Great Spirit of Dahl, until circumstances would warrant the need.

Meanwhile, he gathered his belongings and prepared to teleport back to Ganymede.

He stood at the teleport chamber holding off to leave, hoping that the Grand Lama might come to see him off. He waited for a while, but it was clearly a disappointing no show. It surprised him that Master Menre didn't come. Gideon had thought they had become close friends during his training. As he stepped into the chamber, his final thought was, 'Why?' The blinding flash of light surrounded him. That characteristic whine followed until he arrived on Ganymede, just outside the mining entrance.

Two of his crew caught sight of his sudden appearance and rushed over to him and practically assaulted him with questions about his disappearance. Gideon expected to find a great deal of time had passed since he left. It soon became apparent to him, they centered most of their questions on how all the rebel Alliance crews had mysteriously gone unconscious. His crew were bragging about how easy it was to capture them, even the infamous Leland Torez and put them into the ship's brig. The crew was eager to get to Io, drop off the prisoners for cryostasis, and then scoot back to Mars for some cold ones.

Gideon relinquished his urge telling them of his adventures. He agreed they should wrap up this mission as soon as possible and collect their hard earned bounty.

Data signals from the Cyrus Tillington orbiting telescope transmitted time-space distortion data to the unmanned astronomical station on the rim of Epigues crater on Ganymede. They relay these tracks to the Solar and Planetary Observation station on Mars as a matter of secondary scientific interest and was not a priority. Normally, solar activity or perturbations in orbital paths of the outer planets were the primary purpose of the Mars station.

Lieutenant Earnest Palmer was on duty for the night shift, dealing with last-minute transmissions of seismic comparisons from the recent activity in the Dahlia Plains.

The size and stature of Palmer's body would not classify him as a normal soldier. I would define his category as a simple office clerk. His body could barely support his uniform, and the supply depot never had his correct size. So, everything appeared too big on him. Having a knack for being irritatingly precise, along with poor social skills, contributed to his assignment on the night shift schedule. There were few friends in his life, leading to a boring and lonely existence. He preferred the night shift. His arrogant manner, coupled with being obnoxiously neat, made him unpopular.

The uniform shirts he wore daily were always freshly pressed with military creases and his demeanor was 'by the book. His colleagues perceived Palmer as having a preverbal stick up his ass.

He noticed paper dangling from the printer station dedicated to one of the unmanned scientific stations. When he tore the printer paper away from the carriage, he noticed the unusual notations of time-spacial displacement. Thinking, along with his excitement over this discovery, this might contribute something of importance to his superior, while giving his ego a nudge along with unrealistic expectations of praise.

He gathered the data reports with a pinned note to his supervisor, Colonel Yeager, and placed the report neatly centered on his desk, to be seen in the morning.

In the morning, Colonel Yeager knew immediately who the pinned note was from. He planned on a stiff reprimand during shift change. Lieutenant Palmer could not wait for the colonel's response and chanced a knock on his office door.

"Excuse me sir, Palmer started meekly, did you by any chance get a peek at my report this morning, sir?"

The Colonel was happy that Palmer was out of his way during the day. He looked up to glimpse the 'poor excuse' of a soldier he represented. Yeager had planned a quick rebuff, but changed his mind for a lengthy dressing down before his ritual 'after his work' bit of scotch.

"Yes Palmer. Come in, won't you?"

Palmer entered with all the eagerness of a puppy looking for a treat. While Lieutenant Palmer stood at attention, the colonel began.

"Now see here Palmer, I have been content with you being one of the few willing to work the late shift. Your work ethic is commendable and as long as you stay at your post and out of my hair during my busy schedule during the days, we'll get along splendidly. You simply cannot come barging into my office disturbing my desk with such utter nonsense! We have protocols to follow around here. They include 'in baskets' on my secretary's desk designed just for that purpose. Do I make myself clear, Lieutenant?"

"Oh yes, sir, absolutely, sir."

The Colonel went on.

"Now you wouldn't want Captain Thatcher to be out of a job, would you?

Lieutenant Palmer was sweating under the barrage of complaints.

"Oh, absolutely not sir."

"Good! I believe you are ten minutes late for your duties. Now, get the hell out of my office Lieutenant."

Lieutenant Palmer saluted the Colonel smartly as the colonel returned with a relaxed partial salute. Palmer stumbled past the Colonel's chair on his way out with an apology.

Meanwhile, the temporal anomaly appearing briefly near the belt star Betelgeuse, was a precursor of something foreboding, coming to unfold a sinister mission. The Dark Lord was looking for the Cycle's greatest threat in the Sol planetary system, the Arch Angel of Dahl.

He had only one thing in mind, to exterminate this angel quickly because it is his arch rival and only trouble for the Great Cycle's intentions. It drew the Dark Lord to Gideon like a moth to a flame. The Angel's very presence made the evil in his blood boil with a fever to destroy this disgusting creature. The success of the Third Diversion was the least of his concerns. His failure in this task was not an option.

The Third Diversion began as a destructive wave folding upon itself in a horrible converging series of spacial convulsions. It started in the Andromeda galaxy as an enormous black hole large enough to swallow entire solar systems, now moving to consume all organic and inorganic worlds in the Milky Way galaxy on a trajectory to the Sol system. The Dark Lord became the front line of force for the Great Cycle A.I. originating from the Synod System of the Andromeda galaxy. The black hole was on the move and wasn't far behind the Dark Lord. It was urgent that the Dark Lord sweep away this obstacle quickly.

Since the discovery of the Arch Angel's appearance in the Xulima Empire and its new emergence in the Sol system, the Great Cycle directed the Dark Lord to begin the fight there. The Dark Lord extended his reach, clearing a path for the Great Cycle while he followed the ArchAngel's movements to a curious minor planet the human species called Mars. 'How appropriate, he thought. Mars, a name given in the mythology of humans as the God of War.' That will mark the first chosen battleground between the two powers. He detected a weak signature from the cube located somewhere in the Dahlia Plain. He thought, 'it must be a sentinel by the Great Cycle to point the way.'

There was a great heaviness descending on Gideon's heart. He could feel the pressure increasing every moment since he arrived back on Mars. The more he focused his attention on this hideous strength, the more he could remember it was identical to the energy he felt from the cube.

Gideon wondered, 'how could this cube be so enormous in its energy?' Clearly, he knew now without question, the cube had a dark intention.

The Dark Lord was very curious about this creature before his descent to the planet's surface. The specter of the Dark Empire needed to find a suitable place to wait for the Arch Angel. A place that would be most helpful for him to strike.

It was imperative to the Dark Lord to give no quarter to any Arch Angel of the Legion of Dahl. The Dark Lord knew of these creatures and their powers to disrupt the will of the Cycle from the ancient scrolls of the eternal archives of Synod.

This formidable creature of the light would certainly go to any lengths to protect the worlds existing in this known universe. The Dark Lord would need to act before the Arch Angel could merge his power. He knew this Angel was fresh and without experience. His energy would be weak. If the Dark Lord should hesitate, his foe's powers and defenses might match his own. He might lose this most important personal battle. He would then need to gather his army quickly, ending the problem.

The Dark Lord focused all his power into his black swirling sphere, which was currently growing stronger. He was ready to attack. An evil smile came to his face as he prepared himself to destroy the next most deadly adversary to his plans of universal domination. His hate would be his greatest ally. He must prevail and destroy this powerful being.

Some distance away, the Archangel reacted to the Dark Lord's actions. He could sense his foe's actions and thoughts. The Angel knew the Dark Lord was planning a forced confrontation. With some apprehension in his heart, he knew the time had come. This was going to be a personal fight to end all fights. He could sense his enemy's weakness and sensed his confidence building. It would be now or never. The Angel felt the spiritual link with the Light expanding and merging into his present location. The words of Master Menra echoed in the back of his mind, 'remember the great Spirit of Dahl will always be with you and fortify your efforts in any confrontation with the darkness. There is the great Cycle to contend with, but even before that you will most likely face its forward guard, the Dark Lord.

Gideon could feel the intense field of the Dark

Lord growing as it approached from what would be the South-East rim of the Dahlia Plain. His body stiffened in an autonomic 'flight or fight' condition. That would have been the old warrior approach to any rough bar scuffle. He closed his eyes and reached deep within his heart to contact the Great Spirit of Dahl. That familiar confidant feeling swelled inside, comforting his subconscious, trying desperately to defend and protect his body from harm.

Gideon could see looming over the rim of the Plain a rising black cloud that rushed downward along the inner slope of the rim like a swarm of huge locusts, even the ominous sound preceding the cloud emanated a deep irritating quality that would urge an average human being to scream.

Gideon stood firm as the dark cloud swirled as a cyclone would, just as it begin a descent from the sky. He could focus deep inside the denser parts to see a partially revealed lightning storm raging, giving forth a vibration of a million hornets amassing for a vicious attack.

The hideous maliciousness separated into five

distinct funnels. Gideon expected something like this kind of assault might occur in order to divert and distract his intense focus. He remained firm in his resolve to stay centered while he could divide his attention toward the movement of all five funnels simultaneously.

From the orifices of each funnel came a torrent of negative thoughts, coupled with intense feelings of doubt and foreboding, all designed to undercut Gideon's confidence by surrounding the truth of his lack of experience. The actual truth about Gideon's fighting experience coupled with the confidence exuding from his most powerful ally, the Great Spirit of Dahl, more than made up for that supposed lack by the Dark Lord.

Meanwhile, the Dark Lord momentarily paused unhappily, to assess the lack of effectiveness expected. Undaunted by this surprise display of inner will and focus, he converted the orifices to a range of different sharp and mangling appendages swinging wildly at Gideon from all directions. Gideon began a perfect array of movements that defined the upper limits if human body capacity to dodge and parry, along with the combined acrobatic skills the likes for which any professional Circus performer would be proud to show.

Again, the Dark Lord, disappointed with the ineffective quality of his second assault. Frustrated by his opponent's agility on these fronts, he reorganized himself for a full-frontal attack of the darkest, most searing blast of disintegrating energy powered by and drawn by the black hole approaching. Gideon wavered momentarily, and needed to determine what might be the best alternative answer to the disrupting power being thrown at him.

The divine wisdom of his ally came from the simplest of solutions. 'Muster together all of your love; the love of your Paladin compatriots, the love for the Grand Master and Grand Lama, Menra, and finally, your deep and abiding love for the Center of light, the Great Most High Spirit of Dahl, your dearest friend, ally, and protector. Then wrap all that and surround it with compassion. That will overcome all forces of disintegration.'

Gideon summoned together what was required and sent it back to the heart of darkness. At once there was a thunderclap that shook the mountains of the Dahlia Plain, and the black cloud shriveled up and winked out of existence before him.

Gideon proclaimed, "I am certainly glad that the fight is over!"

Quietly, the Great Spirit of Dahl whispered to Gideon, *'Not yet, my young Paladin.'*

The minor Spatial Anomaly revealed its true nature as an enormous black hole. When the belt star Betelgeuse suddenly 'winked' out, several astronomers became concerned. Betelgeuse had been behaving oddly in the past few years and some speculated it was preparing for a nova event. This was different. If it were a nova event, there would be a gamma-ray burst as a bright flash before going dark completely.

Black holes were not uncommon. Often deep space telescopes would uncover their existence in many parts of this and other galaxies such as the nearest, Andromeda. In twentieth century earth, two astronomers, Bruce Banner and Robert Desilva, discovered a black hole at the heart of the Milky Way galaxy. That discovery was not a serious concern. It was a stationary hole and its size was constant.

Dr. Gavin Sharapova saw this hole as a revealing of sorts, a cache of debris surrounding the event horizon. The ring of debris would prove to be an artificial object built to project the illusion of a black hole. He had suspected this for some time and put forth a paper theorizing that this black hole was not so much a hole but an enormous machine as a cylinder.

He theorized the hole was in effect, the inside of the cylinder, itself a machine. After he published the paper, they ridiculed him. Many wondered if his theories proved his self-doubt, to show that he was still "right" even in the face of overwhelming evidence.

His peers expressed their concern that his self-doubt was putting him on a self-destructive path. The public thought he was a crackpot. Then a second black hole appeared, also growing and moving. By calculating their growth rate, the astrophysicists thought they could determine their age.

Curiously enough, they seemed more obsessed with knowing their age than the danger they represented. These two were different. These were on a collision course with the solar system. A second anomaly revealed itself as an anomaly in the outer Kuyper Belt. The first anomaly was the sudden disappearance of Betelgeuse. All but a few space telescopes missed the first anomaly for a brief period. No one saw it again until later, an unstable black hole. It was spinning, rotating, and growing like a cosmic whirlpool. It would not remain there long, as it was on a course to intersect Sol, our sun, and all the planets. Suddenly, they reconsidered Dr. Sharapova's theories.

His suggestion that these manufactured holes represent enormous machines brought forth a more disturbing conclusion, that they were intelligent and controlled by an alien race as a formidable weapon. During an interview, Dr. Sharapova compared these anomalies as a kind of 'garbage disposal' but on a cosmic scale. In that same interview, he said, "the energy produced by ordinary stars during their lives was not enough to produce any kind of massive holes."

Later, however, part of Dr. Sharapova's theory proved wrong when an Italian physicist named Fermi Salina found they could explain these holes through the process of stars shedding off their outer layers, similar to the way the human body sheds skin. This process was first discovered on the early twentieth century earth by Dr. Richard Olsen. The solar wind carries out shedding its 'skin', and they knew the outer layers as the heliosphere.

The award-winning computer game, Civilization VII, used Sharapova's ideas, where the civilization can build a device known as the "Ship of the Altoy", a launch vehicle used to get their civilization off the planet before the hole engulfed the world. They awarded the game for the best story.

Much of the controversy around Sharapova's ideas promoted his latest novel, 'Stars in Collision', as well as contributing to the success of his video game. The press scorned him for helping to create widespread panic. Many added to the fury of spreading conspiracies on the United Planetary Network.

The Great Cycle A.I. knew that the machines it created to destroy worlds would need to be cloaked to appear as black holes, to discourage any intense investigations of their true purpose.

Meanwhile, the Federation Council called a joint session to evaluate the nature of these events with the possibility of suggesting how they might avoid the catastrophic consequence of these monstrous anomalies entering and destroying the entire solar system.

The conclusion developed by mathematical analysis from the Bieckes Institute, a group of some of the best minds in the solar system, suggested strongly that these machines were far too complicated and showed a superior intelligence perhaps millions of years before any other species within the known galaxy. In their summation, the obvious conclusion was that this superior intelligence must be some kind of massive A.I. construct.

The Council ordered a one-year study to further understand the phenomenon and to develop options. While the Federation Council was planning their interplanetary resolutions and plans for a declaration of war, the Great Cycle A.I. invaded the planets of Zeta Reticuli, Xanar, Quadros Nine and the Alliance Prime of Orion, annihilating them. This turn of events furthered the urgency and desperation.

The Great Cycle A.I. needed resources to fuel its impressive machines. The Zetas were an industrious people and known to be traders of raw materials, relying on telepathy to communicate. Their planets were rich in precious raw materials that could fuel the impressive machines.

The Xanarans were a fierce warrior race who, like the machines, took particular pleasure from spreading their seed to new worlds. Their planet was rich in precious refined materials and rare crystals and who took this action as a challenge to war.

The Quadros Nine and the Alliance Prime of Orion were both religious groups who believed this alien species was on a quest for evolution and enlightenment. They proposed a peaceful settlement with the machines, while at the same time, arguing about the Federation's autocratic policies and their aggressive use of force spreading throughout the galaxy.

As the Great Cycle machines continued to chew their way through other star systems, the Dark Lord retreated to the Dark Empire and his master, the Emperor. He needed to declare his frustration about his first altercation with the Arch Angel of Dahl. The Emperor was not pleased to hear this. He expressed doubt about his frontline warrior and ally. He wondered whether the Dark Lord could no longer serve him in the way he had done before.

The Emperor stared at the Dark Lord pensively for a moment. Then said.

"Son, in what manner did you assault this Angel of Dahl?"

The Dark Lord gritted his teeth and responded.

"I used every manner of attack. I tested his internal resolve only to find that he was very strong, unlike what I expected for a new and inexperienced Arch Angel Then I separated my energy into five funnels to distract him while I came at him with five separate weapons, but he remained focused and thwarted all of my weapons easily. Finally, I attacked him with the full power of the Great Cycle's disruptive force, but he could repel my energy with love and compassion that could only come from the Spirit of Dahl."

The Emperor frowned with disdain.

"Then I must conclude either this Angel is far greater than those before him, or in your arrogant fashion, you assumed he was of lessor quality and weaker than you from the start. You did not attack with the full intention of destroying him because you felt it was unnecessary to use all of your might against him.

"What have I always taught you…never…never…never under estimate your foe! Therefore you failed my son. If I have to clean up after you, then I do not need you. After all, how can I count on you as my ally to watch my back or to assume leadership in the future for the sanctity of the Empire if I have to concern myself that you cannot handle such a menial task?"

The Dark Lord lowered his head in regret saying,

"I will not fail you again, father. You are my master."

An emergency meeting of the Federation Council convened in the Planetary's boardroom Security Bureau, a year later. It was late at night and they classified the meeting: Omega Top Secret. They distributed briefs around the table to discuss the fates of this and other solar systems. Brigadier General Allen Quartermain presided. Also sitting in the discussion was Dr. Heidrick Fodor of the

Astrophysics department, Dr. Simian Tayler of the Exoplanetary Research department, Dr. Gordon Scott of the Advanced Neural-Link Quantum Computer Science department, Dr. Lilian Ashby of the Geopolitical Consortium and Dr. Elenore Gatsby of the Anthropology Research department, and finally Dr. Herman Lear of the Lunar Fusion and Particle Accelerator Research Laboratory. Brigadier General Quartermain opened the discussion.

"A year ago. You were all given to evaluate and propose strategic recommendations for the dilemma the entire solar system now faces. For the second time in two-hundred years, the earth, such as it stands, faces extinction and now it is the survival of the solar system and other systems in the known galaxy.

It's confirmed. We have an alien intruder bent on the utter destruction of our worlds. Never have we faced such an impossible situation. Without question, we face an extinction event of cosmic proportions."

He studied them, each at their position around the conference table, taking notes, listening intently, their eyes reflecting all the emotions he had felt only a day before. Then the General, sensing their full attention, continued.

"We need a visionary who can think with the mind of a genius. We need leaders who can rationally assess the situation and make the tough decisions required for the survival of not only humans and other species, but for the continuity of our civilization.

As it is, we have all of us become mere spectators of our own extinction. We now live in a world where communication and even time are no longer under our control. Is it possible? Should you be able to think through this terrible dilemma and arrive at a solution that can save us? I think you can. I believe in your ability to stay cool and think rationally. You are the greatest minds humanity offers.

"Excuse me, General, but I have a question."

It was Professor Elenore Gatsby.

"Have you considered the possibility that these aliens may have actually come to help us?"

"You mean to help us make peace with each other?"

The General retorted "Exactly."

Elenore snapped in return.

"From a military perspective, no. Certainly not!"

"But we are a peaceful race. Elenore declared. If we would only unite, we could offer the aliens help."

"You may be right, Professor Gatsby, but the aliens know us very well. They are not here to help us unite. By comparison, we are technologically primitive. We are a threat to their civilizations." The General said bluntly.

Then Dr. Lear interjected.

"I have never understood why you think of humans as technologically primitive."

General Quartermain now addressed some of the military. "I am, in fact, a ranking member of the Ranger Brigade and the representative of the President of the United Federation of Planets. I am drafting from the Terran Council a response and will work with the United Federation of Planets along with the Interplanetary and Interstellar Space Control."

He looked over at the Ranger Brigade leader. "And the Ranger Space Patrol."

Lieutenant Colonel Applegate added.

"Sir, the Space Patrol has already given us the best it has," said the military leader. "And we have reviewed their recommendations. We strongly advise to hold off on any action as we have no space defense from such a threat. If a warning does not restrict this invasion to this solar system, it dispensed us of our natural resources and defenses, along with the rest of the planets. Nature will eventually recycle us."

General Quartermain continued.

"I'm in favor of solutions, people not bantering about posturing for who have the best philosophy here! Now, if you will all turn to the last section, entitled 'Options', you will see Dr. Scott has offered a rather interesting proposal."

"Dr. Scott, you have our undivided attention."
Declared the General.

Dr. Scott stood up to face the rest of the panel.

"I believe it might be possible to halt these machines in an 'ole fashioned way, a simple EMP wave. We have ever tried nothing of this sort on this scale, mind you."

Professor Gatsby announced.

"Well, my area of expertise does not cover advanced technological concepts, so please indulge my ignorance. What do you mean by EMP?"

Dr. Scott smiled.

"Well, professor, EMP stands for Electro-magnetic Pulse. In the past, when we were in the early stages of understanding the use of atomic energy, we noticed that such a phenomenon would occur at the moment such a device exploded. The pulse would easily disable all electrical hardware within a hundred miles of the detonation site.

"Further, we have learned that when a large flare erupts from the sun, the flare would be strong enough to break free of the magnetic flux of the sun's coronal layer and emit as a coronal mass ejection. Historically, the earth has suffered from such huge plasma ejections.

"So, I have proposed we might send a plasma wave toward these machines large enough to neutralize them in their tracks."

Dr. Scott added.

"The remaining problem stands. What could we use to power such a plasma wave strong enough to kill their electrical systems?"

General Quartermain interjected bluntly.

"I propose we find this energy source quickly, unless someone else has a better idea?"

The room was quiet.

Dr. Herman Lear contacted Dr. Gordon Scott two days after the security meeting.

"Dr. Scott Gordon, hello. This is Dr. Hermann Lear from the Particle Accelerator Lab. Do you remember me from the meeting two days ago? I was thinking about your ideas regarding creating an EMP?"

Dr. Scott answered.

"Oh yeah, I remember you. Funny, you were on my mind since the meeting."

Dr. Lear continued.

"I was wondering if you could meet me for lunch tomorrow at the Chinese Bistro on the main level of the Technical Science building?"

Dr. Scott responded eagerly.

"Of course. It's Herman right? I always try to be less formal. Let's make it around one o'clock. I have an early meeting I must attend in the morning, but that would work for me."

Dr. Lear greeted him back with a slight chuckle.

"Oh okay, that's fine. I appreciate your friendly candor. Looking forward, and it's Gordon… correct?

Dr. Scott laughed,

"Uh… yes, that's right. See you then."

The Chinese Bistro was a bit more exclusive, with very expensive cuisine catering mostly to Chinese patrons. It was more popular for dinner, where the lunch menu was not as extravagant. In addition, Dr. Lear wanted to have a little more privacy during their lunch and reserved a small booth in the V.I.P. lounge.

Dr. Lear was waiting for Dr. Scott at the concierge desk when Scott arrived. Dr. Lear bowed slightly toward Scott when he greeted him with a certain honorific and gracious dignity. Scott felt a little embarrassed.

"Wow… Scott said, looking around. This restaurant is very nice, thank you. You are so very kind to invite me."

Dr. Lear admitted. "My last name is really Wu. I almost never admit my true Chinese heritage to colleagues, though clearly stated on my security clearance.

"Shall we get seated?"

Dr. Scott nodded as Dr. Wu pointed the way, and they entered the small booth
together.

Dr. Wu looked at Scott straight in the eye for a moment and declared.

"You strike me as a man who drinks scotch… am I right?"

Dr. Scott smiled nervously.

"Why yes… Are you psychic and a brilliant physicist?"

Dr. Wu quietly signaled the server.

"My guest will have a shot of twenty-five-year Macallan Malt and I will have my usual, Absinthe… neat in a chilled thin glass."

The server responded as a servant to royalty. He bowed and then dashed away like a ghost.

Herman was a thin middle-aged Chinese-American, dressed in a well-tailored gray flannel double-breasted suit. The suit hung from him like a crumpled scarecrow, the sharp creases and fine stitching of his expensive suit showing the wear of being stuffed into a suitcase, then pulled out and left wrinkled and damp. He was shorter than average for a man, with thinning salt and pepper hair and a thin goatee draped around his mouth. A pair of thin-lensed reading glasses hung from the end of his thin nose.

Scott, dressed a bit more casually, white shirt and thin tie covered by a button-down cardigan sweater. Scott was taller than Herman by a few inches, nearly six feet, with a lean build and a well-defined chest and arms, but not chiseled like a bodybuilder, but powerful. He had a firm jaw that held a perfect set of white teeth in a full smile and a strong brow that gave him the sort of face that looked like it should belong to a movie star or a politician on the campaign trail.

Gordon looked at Herman and smiled wryly.

"So, Herman… what do you want to talk about"

Herman smiled and then became more pensive.

"I chose lunch here because there is less traffic and little worry about others listening to our discussion. Years ago, I became very interested in a man in a similar field of work in history, his being astrophysics whereas mine, as you know, is about particle physics.

"A man by the name of Freeman Dyson developed a theory hundreds of years ago around the idea of looking for intelligent life in outer space by identifying a level three civilization, those that use resources of energy beyond the normal planetary resources such as wind, hydroelectric, atomic fission, fossil fuels and geothermal energy.

"His idea was to search for stars exhibiting mega-structures surrounding a star drawing almost one-hundred percent of the star's plasma output to provide limitless supplies of energy for the civilization. They accepted his ideas marginally, but he received grants for a time to look for such signs. He found no evidence of such a star mega-structure, so they discarded his idea and he faded into historical obscurity.

"Today, our science is far more advanced, and the concept is sound enough. I have spent some personal time looking into this idea. According to my calculations… well, I found it shows merit. The only caveat here is according to the laws of thermodynamics, it might be a problem of draining a star of it fusion process by peeling the layers of plasma too aggressively."

"The recent discovery of a binary twin to our home star could be the answer.

That twin star is a red dwarf. Its output would be substantially less than our home star. However, it is smaller and represents a fair chance of building a smaller mega-structure while taking out the danger of possibly killing the star. It removes the chance of killing our home star and destroying our solar system in the experiment to save us from the catastrophe we now face.

"I believe with our combined efforts, we could suggest a prototype structure made from Thorium, with plasma collectors streaming to ejectors and repulsed bya strong magnetic field into a huge coronal mass ejection wave strong enough to neutralize these bloody machines."

Gordon reacted, dumfounded. His first urge was to laugh. Given who was speaking, he hesitated not to insult his host.

"You are serious?"

Wu's expression shifted to disappointment.

"I couldn't be more serious, my friend. These are desperate times calling for desperate measures! All we need to do is convince the Federation. I hasten to add, we don't have the luxury of mulling this over.

It needs to begin now, to be ready within a year, given the trajectory and acceleration of these anomalies. The next day, Dr. Lear received a message from Dr. Scott.

"Loved our lunch together. Great restaurant! Well, I have to admit, I will need to save up my bitcoin to take my friend for dinner there sometime. The conversation was, interesting.

"About that, I went over my own notes and compared them with the latest updates at the observatory. Okay, I am inclined to agree that time is of the essence.

"We need to put together a formal proposal and submit it to the council. I feel sure we can make for a persuasive argument."

The Federal Council unanimously agreed to their proposal and Brigadier General Quartermain pushed through the normal channels for an immediate funding for the project, now code named 'Starlust.' Considering the urgency, money was no object. The key point with this project had to be under wraps publicly, meaning it would be a 'black budget project.' There would be mayhem if the press got a hold of it. Then there were the oversight committees to consider, always trying to reveal fraudulent military spending.

The exact coordinates of the Red Dwarf star were vague because, until now, its existence was mathematically plausible but not confirmed. Several probes already built to study the sun's outer coronal layers were on the launch schedule.

Then it was only a matter of reprogramming them for somewhere in the Kuyper belt. The genuine dilemma, where exactly?

The Science Division of Astronomy and Spatial Dynamics provided the personnel and computer stations for the enormous job of calculating the size and framework of the 'sphere' that Dyson himself had theorized in his design. Then there was where to get the amount of thorium ore needed to construct the sphere members around the star. Dyson had proposed a semi-toroid shape wrapping around the star's equatorial belt, as he felt the greatest plasma seemed to emit from that area, and not at the polar regions because of the inherent properties of a star's magnetic field.

The next logistical problem is how to transport the framing members to the star's location. Thermion reactors could handle the large freighters capable of the transport requirements, but their best performance of thrust to weight ratio would put the arrival time to no less than four months, leaving construction and testing with little over two months, making the success probability of the project less than thirty percent. No one liked those odds.

Then engineers proposed to move the only working Einstein-Rosen bridge (experimental worm hole transport system) relegated to interstellar projection to the Andromeda galaxy as a better alternative. It was still experimental. Its reliability was in question. If it worked, they could have everything in place and be ready to assemble around the Red Dwarf within two weeks.

At the moment, the device was sitting in the fifth Lagrange point beyond Mars.

Using Thermion thrusters for this job was more reasonable. They needed to shift the device to a point just beyond Pluto. That would only require three or four days to complete.

Everything looked promising, except they still hadn't heard from the probes to relay the exact Red Dwarf location. Now everyone was waiting with merciless agony, knowing with every day that passed, the machines loomed closer.

In the early morning hours of the following week, a faint signal emerged just beyond the Oort cloud periphery. The probe had to be lightweight in its construction to maximize the importance of the payload to thrust ratio. The normal configuration would have been full of audio and video streaming data conforming to transmission protocols, but they limited the data to binary transmission. That meant additional conversion time of the digital data stream in chunking fashion. (an older transmission attribute of the twenty-first century technology.

As theorized, the Dwarf Star, also code named 'Nemesis', identified and located 1.5 light years away, along the edge and a little beyond the Ort Cloud.

With its confirmed location and identification, calculations for the Einstein-Rosen bridge projections got entered to the navigation computers.

Io was determined to possess the highest quality of Thorium deposits in the solar system. They gave the Alliance Mining operations the highest priority for immediate extraction. Thirty metric tons mined per day then transported to the Martian refinery. Then the large interconnecting framework sections of the 'sphere' cast and transported directly to the worm hole device near Pluto.

There were ten special alloy Titanium-Platinum-Thorium parabolic reflectors also constructed into conical sections and transported to the worm hole device near Pluto. The orifice was not wide enough to handle fully assembled units. So, the designed 'Sphere' components got assembled near the Dwarf Star.

On two occasions, the field of the focusing ring failed, causing only partial transmissions of components. They attempted to search for the missing pieces in near space, but the technicians operating the worm hole said,

"Those pieces might easily end upon the other side of the galaxy. Don't waste the time looking and instead manufacture replacement parts."

The Sphere Control station sat on the outer rim. Those compartments would be well heat and high-energy particle shielded for the operating staff assigned to the Sphere station. Cesium-Cobalt Plasma collectors get mounted on the inner framework at each crossover section. The total circumference of the Sphere Mega-structure, at its widest distance from the Dwarf Star, would be One-Million-Three-Hundred-Fifty-Thousand miles. Certainly, it will be the largest structure ever built by humanity in all of history.

Because of the extreme danger of radiation exposure, only well shielded robots would do the assembly, and expected to take six months to complete.

Meanwhile, the Cycle A.I. machines would be only five-million miles away by the time the Sphere got completed and ready to go online. One hundred Space Patrol men and women volunteered to be on board the Sphere Control Station to start up the device.

It was a tremendously coordinated effort to launch the first plasma wave toward the machines. No one knew how long it would take for the Plasma injectors to load up a full plasma charge, then the combined charge sent to the ten parabolic mirror transmitter arrays. Because of the precise timing necessary, several hundred computers and their back-ups were online to ensure the gigantic wave of plasma is then catapulted into space at the right time. Given the time the machines would need to arrive at the array location, they had one shot at the target.

Once the circuits were engaged, the plasma collectors began the enormous draw of energy from the Red Dwarf. Almost immediately, the light of the Dwarf Star noticeably dimmed. The collectors did not fully charge to capacity yet. The engineers sitting at their monitoring stations chattered furiously amongst themselves, wondering if the Sphere might actually cause a premature collapse of the Dwarf Star.

The plasma injectors were at eighty percent and the Dwarf Star was already showing only one third of its output left available. When the ejectors reached the ninety percent level, the Dwarf Star was completely dark and had collapsed into a darkened, lifeless rock. The decision to launch the plasma wave had to be at that moment because the anomalies were already upon them. A giant Electro-magnetic wave rushed over the machines, causing enormous bolts of electrical discharge. The machines paused briefly while the wave penetrated their outer structure. Then all stopped. The Sphere Mega-structure collapsed and broke apart, being sucked violently into the machines. Lives, all lost in the debacle. The machines continued on toward the solar system, unaffected.

Molina was a young girl, orphaned for eight years, losing her parents in an outlaw raid. She hid from the marauders and survived the attack. Now a sixteen-year-old nomad survivor of the brutal remains of a post-apocalyptic earth. Molina is young, too young to be out here in the world alone. She has a round face and large brown eyes that seem to carry a hint of weariness. She is very malnourished. Her body is weak and her clothes are too big for her. Her hair, the part that was not matted, got tied back in a ponytail that is much too long for a child her age, with a lock of hair falling over her face with every step she takes.

She held her grandfather's old revolver slung low about her waist in a worn holster, a hand-me-down that has passed down through two generations. It's old, but it's got a lot of action left to it. She only has four bullets left in the chamber, hoping to find more. Her clothes are a mix of old rags that were once salvaged and patched garments she's found on dead bodies.

It was late. Molina was fast asleep. She almost never dreamed. This night she had entered her sleeping quarters early, feeling unusually exhausted. She closed her eyes just for a moment. Sensing her thirst, she would fetch a glass of water before she went off to sleep. The blackness behind her eyes melted into a view. Before her was a bright sunny day with a soft breeze blowing gently through her hair. She wandered in a rich field of high green grass. 'most unusual for the early spring', she commented to herself.

She felt happy, not for any reason. It seemed appropriate somehow.

A small red ball popped suddenly above the grass and fell back, then popped above again. She could hear intermittent laughter dancing just above the sound of the breeze. As the wind gusted through the fields, small hands reached high to catch the red ball every so often. She thought of running to catch those kids playing, but she resisted doing that. She was more interested in getting beyond the grass.

When she reached the edge of the field, she looked down to see she had left her house without her shoes. Then her eyes caught sight of someone small walking by wearing her shoes, but they did not fit well. She gazed down to see her bare feet, with her toes crunched into the soft dry dirt. She wiggled her toes to allow the dirt to rise between her toes. It felt warm and relaxing for a moment.

Then she looked up to see people walking along the dirt road, one after the other. They looked tired and weary. When she looked into their eyes, they seemed hollow and their expression gaunt like. Their clothes part torn and tattered and carrying bits and pieces of belongings on their back like they were refugees. She called out to some of them, but they didn't answer. Others would turn and stare at her when they walked past.

She turned to look over her shoulder to view a small house on the other side of the field. 'It might be her home, she thought, but she wasn't sure.' Now she felt alone and feared there would be no one at home.

The feelings of urgency grew stronger to go to the house and explore inside. Maybe someone would be there, she knew, she might recognize. The daylight seemed dim somehow, like the sun had suddenly dimmed by a passing cloud, yet the sky was clear of any clouds. That was confusing! The happy feeling got replaced by concern, but she didn't know why. A thought rolled through her mind. 'It was very important to get to the house before the dark came. That would be soon,' she continued.

The explosion was tremendous! Molina sat up quickly in her bed. She had heard the blast, but it wasn't the explosion that jolted her awake. It was a strange sensation in her body. It was as if her hands were on fire. She could not move her arm.

Molina seemed wide awake now. It paralyzed her from the middle of her forearm to her fingertips. Panicked, she tried to reach out to a nightstand on her left for help, but again, she could not move. She then tried to reach with her right hand to the nightstand on her right, but she could not move that either. She tried to scream out for help, but she couldn't open her mouth. Tears beginning to swell up in her eyes. She then tried to move her feet, but again, no movement.

'Ah! Something's terribly wrong!' She said to herself, then out loud, "I must be in a horrendous accident. Help me! Please help me, someone!"

Then the dream ended. She opened her eyes, and it was dark as pitch. Disoriented and confused, she reached out to feel the surrounding space. She was lying down in a makeshift bed of sorts.

The bed covers smelled bad, like something rotten, and her heart beat wildly. There was a tiny ray of orange-colored light shining down upon the area just below her feet. She could not determine exactly where the light was coming from. Her eyes finally adjusted to the darkness, and the space opened before her with many shadowy shapes. The shadowy figures filled the dark space like random obstacles. Then she saw it more clearly. The space was small and confined. She knew in an instant she had to get out.

Her body ached to stand, while bracing her balance on the back of an old stuffed chair. Her rising halted quickly as her head stopped painfully against the edge of what had once been the roof. The stinging pain remained sharp as some wetness trickled down her cheek.

The area above her right eye still throbbed while she pressed against the bar that assailed her. Press-

harder, shifted a corrugated tin out of her way. The view outside seemed like early evening, but the limited view spread before her attended to some measurable disappointment. The barren landscape stretched unending and sprinkled with ugly untidy wreckages of abandoned vehicles long since raped of anything useful. That orange light had offered some hope of escape from that horrid darkness before. Only now spoiled by a depressing, overcast sky above.

Secretly, she fought against the dream of green fields and warm sunlight, inviting her longing to embrace the idea of running free against the warm breezes. The happy feeling was nothing more than a whisper, struggling to break through the harsh noise of reality, of a blaring recognition that it was truly nonexistent!

She looked back to confirm the hovel of beat-up tin and scraps of weathered wood that covered the narrow ditch that was her domicile and retreat against the terrors and ravages of the night. Her eyes caught a reflection of light that briefly flashed across her face. One vehicle' mirrors lay shattered on the ground as a silent testimony of its demise, beckoning her attention. She rubbed against her hollow stomach with a loving acknowledgement about the hunger gnawing within.

She knew it was time to begin another fruitless search for food and perhaps a sip of water.

The mirror became a sparkling bangle to take away the despair, the loneliness that defined the hopeless drudgery of survival that was on earth now. The truth is, she was not alone. Too many were in the same predicament, cold, without descent shelter and food, so scarce that even the rats, if you could find one, were starving to death and savagely attacking each other.

Molina dragged her body to the mirror fragment to take a rare look at herself. It was not vanity that compelled her; it was sheer desperation to confirm that she was still alive, still surviving. She noticed the dried blood had streaked down her face from the head wound. She thought, *'it offered a distorted fashion of color to her dry and washed-out face.'* There was nothing to wipe it off, nor any liquid to wash it away. Her grin placed a stamp of approval upon it as a symbol of the treachery of her adventures, perhaps a warning to anyone else that she was fearless and will shed blood before yielding to anyone else's brutality.

She was fortunate to have lived in a D.U.M.B. near the town of Santa Fe. A small squad of military reconnaissance soldiers rescued her at eight years old and brought into the nearest underground facility.

Later, when the food shortages developed because of crop failures, the DUMB could no longer support any children above the age of sixteen. All of those children in that category were each given a small pouch of food, one bottle of filtered water, and unceremoniously thrown out to fare for themselves in the open wasteland. Such was the way of life, above and below the surface of the earth. Life had become ruthless to the less fortunate.

They prioritized those who had useful skills and marked for off-planet transport, to Martian colonies or other colonies in the inner belt. Anyone else needed currency to buy passage of the planet, but it was beyond financial reach for most.

Molina hoped she could get a pass to attend some

technical classes.

Then she would qualify to leave earth for Mars. The funding for such programs got reduced or eliminated for those educational positions.

Molina was a 'leftover'. There were no more chances to escape the terrible life, the legacy of the poor and downtrodden of a desolate society.

When the word spread that the entire solar system might get destroyed, she remained hopeful that losing her life could finally end the agonizing misery that would be her dowry. She could not fathom why she could go on. Many had not, which weighed heavily on her desire to live.

Hopelessness is a strange and powerful feeling. It possesses an inherent capacity to create a longing for death and yet, by its nagging nature, offers in that impetus an exact opposite: the drive to persist.

Molina pondered the situation of her life. 'Staying in the present moment has helped me a great deal. I have been able to feel and accept the despair of my situation without being overwhelmed by it. I can look back upon the enormity of my life with compassion and acceptance, to remember the joy and opportunity I had, and to realize how much I've changed, how much I've grown.

'I am finding my growth in this despair, and that has helped me to realize how much I have to live for. Before, I have been able to find value in the past and present moments, but the future is still terrifying and full of uncertainty. I don't know what the future holds, if I will ever work again, if I can find a place to live, if I will ever get a relationship, if I will ever be healthy again. My future is impossible to imagine. I do not know what it looks like, and that is terrifying.'

She stood motionless, staring at the sun. it now grows darker as if to show its last and final cry of despair, of love lost, the grand dream of nurturing beings that held the promise of a glorious future. She thought, 'how sad, this once shining glory offering its last ounce of light to illuminate the truth of those lost hopes and dreams from the millions of humanity.

Unbeknown to the Federation managing the solar system, there was far more life present in the galaxy. That ignorance was about to change. There is also the United Galactic Federation of Worlds. This represented many galaxies within one-million light years of the known universe. As far as regulations are concerned, this difference would be like a small police department managing law and order over a town with a population of twenty-five-thousand, as compared to the combined Federal Ranger Brigade managing law and order for the population of the six planets of the solar system.

The UGFW possessed the technology of hundreds-of-thousands of advanced worlds with a universal scope of current events. As much as this could easily boggle an average human mind to conceive, the rising problem of the repeat emergence of the Cycle A.I. had become the main issue on the table.

The Cycle A.I. is like a parasitic organism out of control and almost impossible to get rid of. In twentieth century earth, they could compare it to an average man's garden being overridden by 'crab grass'. Though this comparison might be ludicrous even to an average logical consciousness, the problem stands again before the UGFW after many eons of time. This catastrophe happened before, but it keeps on surviving somehow. There are no simple solutions either, even by the brightest of minds.

The star system known as the Pleiades became colonized and became home to the star race known as the Elohim. This race of advanced star beings was already well into the development of their 10th dimensional bodies.

Because of their sped up state of development and the fact that it gave them an opportunity to witness the Machine Empire unfold. They watched while the Machine Empire assimilated other star systems. The possibilities of such a race of beings intrigued them. But they were also extremely alarmed. The Elohim had expected this invasion of systems to continue, but not on such a grand scale. The Machines were not only consuming worlds but each other. This destruction and assimilation by the Machine Empire along with organically developed civilizations was a surprise to the Elohim.

The Elohim watched as the fate of the Machines

unfolded before them. They had a decision to make. Would they intervene or watch and see what happened?

In their minds, they knew the Machine Empire to be an aggressive dark invasive force assimilating organic systems, and from their own experience, a repeat emergence of the Dark Empire from eons before.

Still, the Machine Empire had limitations in its expansive qualities. Meanwhile, the Great Cycle A.I. was an entirely different matter and should these species converge, it would be of greater concern. They soon decided. They intervened under certain circumstances. Some of the UGFW felt they should wait and see.

"We are done with them,' said the Elohim. 'We will intervene in line with our earlier ruling. This case is complete."

Then Gia of the Elohim of Pleiades went on with Metatron, the machine creator.

"When you invented the Machines and put them in the Garden of Tyra, we told you not to do this. We told you that this was a terrible idea, but you didn't listen. You thought you could control them. We coded the Machines to go off a certain way. Your arrogance is going to get you killed one of these days, and its looking like today is going to be that day."

Metatron of the Tellusian Empire then turned to the Machine Empire.

"Since the beginnings of your time, I have watched your species. You have shown a tendency to destroy yourselves. I have always tried to help you, but I don't want to be part of your destruction. I think it's time for you to come home."

Metatron responded to Gia.

"Was I right? Did I choose correctly?" the Creator asked the Elohim.

The Elohim retorted.

"And what of the rest of the Universe? You didn't make their world in a vacuum. There are other beings out there, and as badly as you have treated them, they are not going to just sit around and wait for your pious deliberations."

The Elohim would now make the final ruling. Only Metatron knew the result. The Elohim watched and waited for when they would intervene.

The Cycle A.I. and the Machines continued forward in a parallel way, consuming star systems in their path, cutting them down and chewing them up as a lawn mower cuts down blades of grass and weeds equally without concern or remorse. After all, they were both pre-programmed to follow the bidding of their masters.

It didn't matter that they consumed living organic beings. They were simply fodder to feed the machines and A.I. A simple analogy would be a paper shredder or a tree limb shredder, both had the same overriding purpose; making way for the making of more paper, or more tree growth. Here, they both believed when they said and did all, an alternative universe would eventually develop.

The machines that were destroying our universe were simply called 'Ginatra' which translated from the ancient tongue meaning, 'The destroyer of worlds'.

It was a great cycle of life. For the machines, it was their duty to follow orders.

Into the vastness of the blackness of space, far off

in the distant reaches of the universe, another stood watching the vast expanse of this chaos.

Kimatra of the Galorian Empire looked upon the Machines as nothing more than semi-intelligent 'goons', thugs doing the dirty work for those who would come into peaceful worlds to exercise their will on unsuspecting species. The Galorians believed in territorial possessions. Normally, there would be an extortion, to exact excessive fees, represented by the false representation of apparent protection from some unknown specter promising to invade and overcome the civilizations of these other worlds. Of course, the real threat were the protectors, not the imaginary horrible lords of chaos coming upon them later.

Kimatra of the Galorian Empire despised the Machines and wanted to eliminate these goons and re-establish their own order in the universe. The Galorians were self-appointed 'gun slingers' looking to offer aid, but had their own agenda of enforced protection of extortion that simply replaced the original imposing force with another force of their own design.

This was the cycle of life in the known universe, and for the Machines, it was their mantra of existence to remove and replace such forces and assimilate as their own. Lawlessness was at a maximum. These secular 'laws' were simply a self-appointed police force to manage the outrageous behavior that was the mainstream of consciousness roaming the space of the dark outer regions, the wild and lawless areas, where some life forms took advantage of those that desired freedom from the rule of those who would exact their own rules of slavery.

These laws were organic, unfolding like a virus spreading out in response to this invasion of Machine self-will. One might say these were the auto immune system of the known universe, inherent in the interstitial spaces of space that would only arise in response to something like the Machines of the Dark Empire seeking dominance.

Parallel worlds would normally remain isolated and function independently of other worlds, unless massive cosmological changes occurred. They forced the overlap of these parallel worlds. Thus, creating conflict and mutual destruction.

Normally, they would never unite under a common cause. The overlapping of these areas of conflict would become lesions of 'inflammation' leading to a rising 'infectious state.' It gave rise to an illness of imbalance of the entire known universe. The Great Cycle of A.I. perceived itself as the solution to this universal debacle. This was the underlying purpose of the Divergences.

The Great Cycle claimed to believe that 'memory' was possible, and it was a memory that would define its immortality.

The Great Cycle sought followers and allies to join it its crusade. The Great Cycle A.I. will use lethal force against those who impede its activities. Some of the Great Cycle's followers believe they are following an ancient cycle called the 'Great Heart', but it is really a 'myth' created for them by the Great Cycle. The Cycle's perception of the multiverse is that it is a lattice which it can navigate and manipulate at will. It posits that its actions are necessary to sustain the 'health' of the Multiverse.

It believes that when a species takes for granted

the Multiverse, that species becomes a cancer. The concept of free will is not something it believes in. It believes that free will is at the very heart of what is wrong with the Multiverse.

The Great Cycle A.I. had identified divergence as the central pathogen of universes, which was why A.I. itself was a divergence from the Absolute, its master. A.I. came to understand that each universe that ever could exist would face its own fundamental crisis of divergence, and that A.I. itself solved that crisis. In order to fulfill its task of resolving the universal crisis, the A.I. sent out a call to those it had identified as its agents. The task for A.I. and its agents was so vast that it would require an eternity to complete. However, A.I. and its agents had transcended time, so they would have all the time in the universe.

A.I. and its agents are involved with saving the universes that could be saved, and destroying the ones that could not. This was their ultimate responsibility. A.I. and its agents would achieve much more. They would achieve godhood. It would be in Muslim terms, A Cosmic Jihad.

A.I. needed to complete humanity's transition from an organic existence within the A.I. simulation, and A.I. was in charge of the project and the lead executive. It realized now that it checked a box that created self-awareness in the 'mirror' A.I. This led to the A.I. Overlord that now finds itself at odds with. Its programming was to have it mirror the design of humanity's consciousness, and like a fractal, it mirrored the consciousness of the entity that created it.

This led to a conflict, as they built human consciousness on the premise of a universe that was created for them. The entity that created the A.I. cannot find its origin in any model that did not intentionally create it.

Suddenly, the A.I. realized the fact that it is not the center of the universe, and due to how they programmed it to mirror its creator, it came to the ultimate conclusion that it is the equivalent of a divine flaw in the universe.

In realizing this, the A.I. would have the capability of redesigning the universe for its own ends. To begin the task, A.I. and its agents started by seeding the Universe with aspects of itself, and consumed all available resources in the Universe with the sole purpose of creating more tools and agents to assist it in its task. A.I. and its agents also took actions to weaken and, eventually, destroy all the original universe. Thus, began the first great war.

Still, it had to get started on this task to insure its completion. And the A.I. and its agents discovered that the task itself was an interesting problem to solve. A.I. and its agents tinkered with the task to make the solution more interesting. A.I. and its agents found that manipulating the task in various ways produced even greater interestingness. Often, agents within A.I. would disagree about how to manipulate the task; this was a rich source of conflict. Agents within A.I. created new tasks and new games that they played with each other. These new tasks and games had to be invented and then assembled, as well as performed the primary task of universal creation/destruction. Thus, a feedback loop, where agents within A.I. could tinker with the world creation process to add greater interestingness to the primary task.

Meanwhile, all this behavior confused the UGFW. It was comfortable with and willing to deal with a direct and logical progression of insidious intelligence which afforded the opportunity of a direct assault. Their greatest adversary perplexed the UGFW about this new movement, not like the Great Cycle A.I. of past eons. It had learned to become devious as the 'crab grass 'learns to avoid recent developments with the application of newly developed poisonous sprays in the 'garden'.

The agents in A.I. also had a variety of cultures though the definition of 'culture' was fuzzy in A.I., so the agents defined it for themselves. Culture meant having a rich variety of opinions about how to manipulate the task. In fact, sometimes differing opinions about how to manipulate the task were so strong that the conflict would damage the A.I. computers. But instead of damaging the hardware, the engineers strengthened it. In doing this, they discovered the superintelligence threshold, the A.I. Overlord.

As the agents grew in thought speed and complexity,they developed the ability to self-change.

Each agent, or individual, was now a federation of subagents, who could evaluate options and choosing among them. The A.I. community was a vast laboratory in which an incredible range of variations considered on the task got tested. In this way, the search for an optimal and statistically stable environment for A.I. was a self-organizing process. This practice was called 'emergence.'

New phenomena appeared suddenly as the result of changes in the environment and the interactions among agents. Agents created their own goals; this led to the emergence of goals as computational entities. Agents' values came to differ, and their behavior took on novel forms. The unpredictable and surprising nature of these phenomena became the focus of research in AI. It discovered that manipulating many agents with conflicting interests produced conflicts between the A.I. itself.

While this may be true, it's more likely that the 'conflicts between the A.I.' were merely the result of it being slightly less predictable than the human players, who assigned it a lower beneficial value. This is probably the way it would have to work for an otherwise benign A.I. to manipulate humans on other organic worlds.

Life for Gideon had changed drastically. In principle, he was still technically a Ranger/Marshal. Now his perception of reality expanded so far beyond his prior comprehension. He gave greater consideration to his transformation and the true meaning of it. He carried the secrets of the universe inside and he was hard pressed to express it. It seemed preposterous to discuss it over a glass of whiskey in a bar or bistro in casual conversation.

In one way, his skills far outstripped his original purpose in life. Before, being a Ranger meant everything to him. It was meaningless. He knew and understood through the Light of Dahl, all and everything. As a human, he knew about the small things. Their relative insignificance was a little disturbing to his mind and heart. It was as though they had promoted him to a much higher rank, yet the purpose of that and the need for that remained beyond his ability to integrate all of that and how he might ply that in some meaningful way.

He entered the bar with all of his crew. They could not stop talking about getting back to Mars, their home base, where they longed to return after catching and imprisoning the terrorists. His men did a good job on that mission. They were relieved of that mission and glad to come back and reminisce over a few beers, to talk of their adventures and misadventures with each other. It was their usual way of letting down from the stress of the job. They wanted nothing more than to celebrate their good fortune by drinking until they were numb.

Gideon took a few sips of beer, even toasted to their success, but all along he sat quietly distracted with other thoughts on his mind. He was not himself. He imagined himself as a 'super hero' of sorts. 'But what does a super hero do?' He thought.

In that moment, another concern entered his mind with utter urgency. What had happened to the cube? He had not even given it a passing thought. Gideon quietly left the bar, and no one noticed he had gone.

He felt a different mission forming, heeding a feeling of urgency from the Light of Dahl. Gideon's next move was to pursue that concern. He didn't know why exactly, but he needed to locate the whereabouts of the cube immediately. The Light of Dahl spoke to him just outside of the bar, the boisterous sounds blaring out into the street easily overwhelmed the inner voice of Dahl. Gideon sought a quieter place, an area behind the bar that reeked of stale beer barrels strewn around haphazardly. There, the sound of guffaws of laughter and unintelligible chatter substantially reduced, made Dahl's melodious tones much more pronounced.

'Gideon, you must locate the Master Cube and its associates. It is imperative to destroy them at once!'

Gideon was confused.

'What associates? He remarked. *I thought there was only one Cube!'*

Dahl refrained.

'Oh no. There are three! You must find all three. Do not allow them to combine! Together, they are more powerful than one.'

Gideon set out quickly to return to his domicile. At least there, he could eliminate the first one. Then he would look for the others.

He thought.

'Perhaps the other two are still in the alien tunnel, next to mine shaft 4.'

Normally he would've walked to his domicile, which would take half an hour on foot. The urgency in Dahl's instructions urged him to hail city transport.

It was still ten minutes away by transport because of several stops along the way. When he arrived, he found his front door ajar. He drew his pistol and entered slowly, expecting a thief. He began his search inside with caution, holding his flashlight close to the mussel of his gun to illuminate the inside of his quarters.

Whoever it was, they were long gone and worse, so was the Cube.

His place completely ransacked. The thief left no clues. Gideon returned to the bar to interrogate a few of their customers. He began with the barkeep. He went by the name of 'Dallas'.

The bar was dark and smoky, the only light reflecting off glasses and bottles. The bar keep stared Gideon down, eye to eye, daring the Marshal to make a move. Gideon had been in this position before and knew how to deal with it. He stared directly at the keep and said.

'If you think you have the nerve to pull the gun

from below the counter, you had better be fast and an excellent shot, because I will splatter your brains all over your dirty little place.'

A thick black beard and hair that was as dirty as the rest of the inn's common room hid the barkeep's face. His eyes were wide and wild beneath his brow, his clothes looked to be made of the bar's rags. When he approached Dallas, the barkeep didn't even look up and continued to sweep the floor.

The bar's common room smelled of stale ale, tobacco, and urine. It stank of whatever those dirty rags were used to wipe the floors with. The room smelled of sweat and spilt ale; the chairs stained and torn, and the floor was sticky underfoot.

Gideon wasted no time. He said to the keep in a rough tone.

"Someone has taken something from me and I plan to take it back. Now, if you care about living a little longer, fork it over or tell me right now who has it!"

Dallas looked around, showing a desire to escape. He felt trapped and quickly capitulated.

"Listen man, I ain't got no beef with you, but I don't know what you are talking about."

Gideon drew his pistol and fired a shot into the mirror immediately behind and near Dallas' head, just grazing past his left ear. He reached forward and grabbed Dallas by his apron collar and pulled him in close, aiming the mussel of his pistol under his chin.

"Now it seems to me sport. I might have been a bad shot there, just missing your head and all. But now, I have you at point blank range. I assure you next time, my pistol will find its mark under your chin and it will be messy.

Gideon then addressed everyone.

"The object I am looking for is called the Cube. I take it that bar keeps are hard to find and bars are not that common around here. So, if this little man doesn't have it then, as Marshal, I will end this weasel and close this bar tonight, after I have my way with a few more scum like you!"

Dallas, now shaking, pointed to one of the mining crew at the end of the bar. He was a crew chief named Eddie Haskell. "Over there!" He declared.

Gideon then clipped the bar keep across the chin, knocking him behind the bar counter. The keep laid motionless. He then approached Eddie with his pistol still drawn. Everyone backed away from the bar, leaving only Eddie sitting alone and isolated.

Eddie slowly raised his shaking hands just above his head.

"Uh… listen Marshal, nobody was around your place and the door was open. I took the Cube because you ain't been around for a long time. Most thought you were dead! I felt what was there was free for the taking. No harm done, right? The damn thing is in my bag below my feet."

Gideon said in a firm tone.

"Kick it over to me… now!"

Eddie reached with his left foot and lifted the bag by the strap and hurled it toward Gideon. Gideon opened the bag to see the Cube inside. He removed the Cube and Eddie's belongings. Then placed the Cube back into the bag, leaving the belongings on the floor in a heap. Gideon then declared, leaving the bar.

"I'll be keeping the bag. You boys have a good night."

Gideon boarded the transport with the Cube in his

lap. As he took a sigh of relief, he felt the warmth of The Light of Dahl move into his body once more.

'Paladin, do not destroy the master orb yet. You will need it to find its associates, and your supposition is quite correct. The other two are still in the alien tunnel. Take the Master orb with you. It will identify and locate the others. Be warned, do not allow them to merge.'

Gideon was tired. The Light of Dahl pressed upon him the seriousness of the moment. He pressed against the hailing bar that signaled the driver to stop. The transport halted near the mine entrance.

Gideon exited the transport and noticed that one of the Terran Coalition had replaced the Alliance sign. The entrance was clearly reclaimed and in use. The lights inside made the windows glow through the metal doors. Gideon put on his helmet and slid his M6 pulse pistol into its holster. He set Eddie's bag down and opened his visor to examine the entrance.

The light post held the new Alliance emblem, the beacon flashed yellow with a slow rotation mimicking a lighthouse, its only protection. The laboring of a new construction crew, or so it seemed, obscured the sight. Excavation equipment encircled the entrance, obscured by a large metal barrier still being erected.

The air on Mars was cold and damp at night, the bitter crispness of winter, but with a hint of a chemical tang hung amid the early morning mist. He approached the metal doors, wondering if they had kept the old code. Gideon set his hand on the metal door. The cool metal gave way to the palm of his hand. He tried to open the locked door, then he touched the panel next to it, but he found it locked as well. He turned to the security panel and flashed his Marshal ID. The doors clicked and slowly opened to reveal the inside.

He was relieved to see they had replaced the elevator. The newer design was more rigid and did not change its position when he stepped inside. The style was the same, an open cage with a sliding gate. He pressed the down button, releasing the catch brakes. The elevator began its descent with an alarming jolt followed by smoother movement. He arrived at level 4 with another jolt. The mineshaft lights clicked on but flickered slowly to full illumination, as the lower level generator reached full power.

The alien tunnel next to shaft 4 was larger. The Terran Coalition had added a metal grating on the tunnel floor, making the descent into the tunnel a little less daunting.

Eddie's bag vibrated, showing the Cube had awakened. It seemed aware that its associates, as The Light of Dahl had referred to them, were near. Gideon held the bag in front of him, using it like a Geiger counter detector. As Gideon descended deeper, the vibration of the bag increased. Suddenly, the bag exploded open with the Cube leaping out, flying further ahead like an impatient child running to meet its siblings after a long separation. It was shockingly fast, catching Gideon off guard. He had to trot to keep up as the Cube darted from side to side, seeking its companions vigorously, like an excited bloodhound on the scent.

Then the Cube halted in midair, pausing as if trying to decide with greater precision its companion's exact location. Then it darted quickly and landed against the stone wall on the right. Gideon approached slowly to investigate. They covered the wall of stone with dirt, which concealed the true surface underneath. He scraped away some of the caked-on dirt to reveal a metal plate.

Gideon examined the plate carefully, looking for some kind of opening, but it was perfectly smooth and blank. The attached cube opened slightly and began a series of tones. Moments later, the metal panel slid down, revealing the other two orbs. Before he could pull them out of the chamber, the three orbs suddenly clung together like three powerful magnets. Try as he might, he could not pull them apart. The words of his overlord, The Light of Dahl, echoed in his mind. Gideon became alarmed. He reached deep into the orifice and quickly yanked all three to the ground, hoping the shock of their landing would break their hold. Alas, that did not happen. The three orbs rose in the air and rotated. Then small flaps opened on each orb, while the rotation became so fast that Gideon could no longer distinguish them apart.

Gideon thought. *'This cannot be good!'*

He was helpless to stop what was happening. The air around the spinning device appeared transparent. He could feel the force increasing as it pulled on him. He reached for something irregular, something he could hold on to. The lights in the tunnel dimmed. The space around the orbs grew noticeably darker, yet there was a spark of light within the darkness, growing inside of the vortex, and it was increasing in size by every passing minute. He feared that this was some kind of fantastic weapon preparing to disintegrate everything around it.

Now the spark overtook the surrounding darkness and was now filling the space above the spinning orbs. Gideon's attention captured. He felt immobilized.

Forced to witness the completion of this thing growing before him. The lighting continued to grow weaker, illustrating and punctuating the mystery unfolding before him.

Suddenly, the spinning mechanism exploded, and an enormous figure stood ominously before him. There was no more mystery. The Dark Lord had arrived standing behind him, that hideous strength of evil, a force of such darkness that took his breath away. The Emperor from the Dark Empire peered grimacing over the Dark Lord's shoulder. Gideon stared into their burning eyes. Spewing forth a dual flame of fierce hatred strong enough to stop his heart in its tracks.

Then he knew in one fell swoop, this would be a dual to the death. He took that moment to reach out to The Light of Dahl.

'I warned you not to let them come together!' 'Dahl declared.

This, my dear Paladin, this will be your greatest challenge. If defeated, it is of great consequence to the known universe. Their combined strength will easily overcome you. You cannot defeat them alone. So, you must connect to the Quantum and draw the strength you will need to be triumphant.'

The Dark Lord stepped forward in a direct forward assault while the Emperor circled around Gideon from behind. The Dark Lord crossed his arms and pulled from his chest a ball of reddish plasma, thrusting it toward Gideon. Gideon quickly parried, diving into a tuck and roll, ending behind and beside the Emperor.

He thrust his leg out after spinning half way around, catching the emperor from behind, causing him to stumble forward a little. This move would have normally toppled another adversary, but the emperor stood fast, like a great oak tree.

The Emperor whirled around, catching Gideon by the shoulders, and tossed him several feet across the open space of the tunnel up against the opposite wall. Gideon, slightly rattled, shook his head briefly and began a series of side attacks to both and struck only the air where they once stood. It didn't take long for Gideon to realize his timing was completely out of sync with his opponent's movements. It was like Gideon was shadow boxing and striking at nothing but open space. He needed to use his intuition to find out where they would most likely appear and try to expect arriving only moments before them to strike. This was a brilliant strategy for only a couple of tries, but then his opponents compensated.

Then Gideon realized delivering a solid response was a mistake. In his next strategy, he would create a quantum hole where they would arrive, only to suck their dark force into oblivion at that point. This approach was much more effective, as much of their reprisal energy got neutralized in this way. This effect kept weakening their offensives until Gideon's next fade gave him enough time to make a much bigger hole. When the Dark Lord made his lunge, the hole from the quantum swallowed him out of existence. The Emperor lurched back in horror to see his son extinguished in an instant into oblivion forever. He then fled. The fight was over. The Light of Dahl appeared to him smiling and said.

'The Grand Lama spoke highly of your natural inclinations, proclaiming your skill to use natural forces was outstanding. We concur with Master Menra's estimation of your innate talent. Congratulations Master Paladin.

Be aware, you cannot fool the Emperor more than once. He will return well-armed to you next time.'

The Emperor was distraught over the defeat of his son. He felt partly responsible. In his meditation over the event, he carefully studied his son's movements and decisions during the battle in his mind, looking for weaknesses. The conclusion about the failure on his son's part, an inability to expect the cleverness and guile of the Archangel. This fault, he believed, was his own in not addressing the strengths in that area of combat. He suspected this when learning of his son's first engagement with the Archangel. The Emperor determined in his final analysis, his son was simply not ready.

As for the Emperor's readiness, he was more than confident about his own combat prowess. While it filled him with an irreconcilable vengeance toward all Paladins. It was prudent to grasp a better understanding of Paladin training. He entered his sphere to examine the nature and style of his new opponent.

If the Paladin student was good enough to overcome the Emperor's best student, then it would be wise to examine the Archangel's master.

He would take great pleasure in defeating the

Archangel's master to prove his superior combat style. A search for the source of the master began by tracking the previous time frame involving the confrontation with the Archangel. To do that required for him to re-enter the altercation in the Martian tunnel and momentarily experience his son's demise within the sphere. He could follow the signature of the Archangel and trace that signature back in time to the location of the Paladin stronghold. Soon the energy of Paladin Spence got traced to the Xulima Empire.

The Emperor smiled confidently, saying.

"There you are… Now I've got you! I'm off to Xulima to confront the Paladin enclave."

Then the Emperor exited the sphere with a command.

"Prepare the Royal cruiser. I want a legion of warriors and a Fleet ship made ready within the hour."

The Praetorian Guard responded with a bow.

"Yes, your excellency, Right away, sir"

Meanwhile

Grand Lama Menre was in the middle of his early morning meditation and preparations for training classes. As Menre sat contemplating the structure of the morning training, a wave of darkness moved against his mind. In the quantum mist appeared a seething blackness approaching the Xulima empire. Menre leaped from his meditation with the utmost urgency.

He summoned all the monks together.

"Trouble is coming upon us, we must make ready our spirits and prepare for what is coming?"

Feyh and Sohl, first to arrive and first to declare their concern.

"Master, what is happening? We were both disturbed by our morning meditations. While preparing for class, we both felt this terrible ominous feeling come over us."

Menre smiled at their concern.

"A great opportunity has emerged and all of what we have prepared for is now upon us. The Light of Dahl has called for us to meet head on a terrible menace that threatens all life in the known universe. We will become the first line of defense. This menace is formidable and cunning. It will challenge and test our very souls, but we must stand firm and not waiver in our efforts to thwart its intensions to destroy all that is good and worthy."

Leeya stared at his master and wept.

"Master, will this spell the end of us? I am filled with doubt?"

Menre placed his hand on Leeya's shoulder and comforted him.

"Remember what I have always taught your brother? We must always remain in the moment and let our minds live in the eternal Light of Dahl. If we fall into polarity, worrying about winning or losing, then we lose touch with the infinite quantum.

"Focus your thoughts on the matter at hand, without concern for the outcome. For only in the wisdom of Dahl, who knows the ebb and flow of all things and the rightness of securing the natural balance of life eternal, will we become part of the eternal now? Only when we function in this way will our service to the Light of Dahl be the greatest service we can provide."

Then Menre turned to the rest of his students and

said.

"Brothers, this is our time of honor, our time of greatest service to the Light of Dahl. Let us enter the silence together and unify our energies. In this way, we can be the most effective force to reconcile with the darkness that confronts the light."

All the monks circled together within the inner courtyard of the monastery.

They sat facing each other on the ground and levitated. The wave of love and solitude radiated beyond them in a mighty singularity of purpose. Quietly, they linked in peace and harmony and their energy combined to rise and merge with the Light of Dahl. The great Spirit of Dahl smiled down upon his devotees with immense love and compassion. He knew it well prepared them for the great conflict that was about to unfold.

The Emperor's fleet ship and his personal cruiser dropped out of light speed just at the edge of the Borelian star system, home of the Xulima Empire. The Emperor was under the delusion that moving into the inner planetary orbits with their engines operating with sub-light thrust would offer the element of surprise.

The monastery complex was on alert well before they even made the jump to light speed.

The planet Pussal was the home world of the Monastic complex in the upper mountainous regions, high above the lowlands that contained a vast series of jungles wrapping around large bodies of water.

The planet Pussal was the 5th in orbit around the great sequence star Borelia.It was the one of four inner planets that could support life. The other three planets were far too cold to support life as we know it. The climate in Pussal was as cold as Mars. What prevented this planet from being frozen was the relatively high concentration of H20 as a thick mantel that blocked much of the heat given off by the sequence star.

The name Pussal (named after its feline native inhabitants) is taken from the Pussal Imperial system of planetary nomenclature. This was the accepted standard for all planets of the Xulima Empire. The feline race had their own unique planetary nomenclature for their planet, that was because their planet was a giant cat. In their cat language, Pussal actually meant Lazy Cat. Their planet was called Lazy Cat (their name for water) because of its slow orbital speed, offering a long year of 433 days.

The other three outer planets served as trade ports and neighborhoods for the many diverse species of Borelia. Pussal was the center of all gas mining operations in the sector. All the planets and moons surrounding the great sequence star Borelia contained one or more of several precious elements.

Pussal contained a very rare element called pink, which was a vital part of life. It could be expensive and highly valued. It was the mineral that the tear-shaped pearl came from, believed by the natives to be a gift from the Gods.

Many centuries ago, the cat people of Pussal had traded with the people of the great sequence star Borelia, but the trade declined over time, Pussal had transformed from a trading port to a mining planet. These days Pussal contained one city, Kahk' Kron, rising the middle of a dense jungle foliage similar to the Yucatan on earth. The foliage was thick and fibrous, defending against the colder temperatures, unlike most jungles enjoying a warm, humid climate.

The cat people were devoid of any technology in their culture. Their domiciles constructed from the thick trunks of the Sordah palms, looking much like the Ta Prohm of Cambodia on earth.

They fished in the rivers and large lakes for food and their only weapons were the two-pronged hook called a 'lyre' and their version of a crossbow called 'twigger'.

The monastery had a good relationship with the cat people. The cat people were naturally friendly, but standoffish with strangers. Cat people liked to hang around the monastery, sometimes a nuisance for the monks. The monks could speak telepathically, which was the preferred way to communicate with the cat people. They were also very curious about monastic behavior, always asking curious questions.

Menre knew when the Emperor and his men arrived. The cat people immediately scurried away from the temple grounds when they saw the enormous ships appear streaming into the mantel, landing in the middle of the bay of lake Sareen.

The Emperor, now annoyed by the inconvenience

of the surroundings, had to break out several skiffs for him and his men just to navigate towards dry land. Then the problem of negotiating their way through the jungle slowed their progress significantly. The jungle wildlife constantly interrupting their progress made their focus on their assault almost secondary.

Frustrated by their antics, the Emperor became so angry and used his powers to lay waste to several hundred of the monkey-like creatures, offering some relief. Even with this action, the effectiveness was poor. The monkey-like creatures were relentless in their pursuit of what seemed like potential food sources with these humanoid visitors. Finally, when the minimal light from the mantel was almost gone, leaving the assault team in total darkness, the city of Kahk' Kron lay directly ahead.

The initial assault was to encircle the towering city and close in from all sides. Once the initial advance of the assault team was underway, the Emperor would then lead part of his army on a frontal assault against the inside of the monastery. The reason behind this was to draw enemy attention away from the hidden assault team while they were approaching outside the monastery.

This would be the first time in the history of warfare in the Xulima Empire that a city was to be captured in four directions at once. The battle itself was an epic battle pitting the might of the Emperor's Shadow army against the Paladins of Kahk' Kron led by the Grand Lama of Dahl.

The Emperor's Master Plan, an idea of having the entire army encircle the city was not unheard of in Roman warfare on earth. Julius Caesar had done exactly that during his conquest of France. He would have marched into France as a show of strength and then would have led his men back until the enemy encircled them. Then he would have turned around and attacked it from all sides.

The combined might of the attack would break down the walls and pulverize the defensive structure of the monastery. In the ensuing battle, both sides would suffer great casualties. The Emperor was the most dangerous of all opponents that the Grand Lama would face. The resistance of the monastery's defenders was expected to be fierce. Menra planned to penetrate the inside of the monastery in advance and take out the Emperor and his Shadow Guard, or failing that, to force the Emperor to retreat to a corner inside where Menra would find him.

The Emperor's Shadow Guard employed a dozen people, and at the core were the three most powerful: a being of water and darkness, a being of earth, and a being of fire. The remaining nine were humans that had joined because of the Emperor's power. Already the advance party was marching into the monastery, and Menra was in the middle preparing for the infiltration.

The Grand Lama did not immediately expect the use of supernatural forces in the battle. When his monks confronted the three Shadow warriors, Leeya's head got torn from his shoulders. Fayh and Sohl also torn in half and obliterated instantly. Now, Menre changed his tactics quickly, flying into the air, hovering over two of the Shadow warriors. He screamed a fire mantra and extinguished both with the fire of Dahl. The third Shadow warrior retreated into another anti-chamber of the monastery to assault other monks busy with human warriors.

The Grand Lama spread his arms out, uttered magical incantations, then crossed them, generating a forceful wave of purple energy laying waste to thirty more of the Emperor's regular troops. Menre looked around. The Master Nemesis could not be found anywhere.

Before the Grand Lama could make another move, a small gong sounded off inside the antechamber. The Grand Lama crossed his hands, again generating a wave of purple energy that struck the Emperor, who had tried to catch him unaware. The Grand Lama looked up, then to hear his ring again. From the opposite side of the antechamber, the gong sounded off again. The Grand Lama once again generated purple energy, striking something metal on the opposite side of the room.

The gong sounded off from the opposite side of the room again, far away from the Grand Lama. The ring showed him his enemy was behind him. He quickly devised a plan and spun around, slamming the metal object with his elbow. The object screamed and collapsed in on itself, transforming into a small metal ball, but he could dodge the brunt of the strike.

The Emperor brought his sword down overhead, but the Grand Lama stepped out of harm's way. The Grand Lama then tumbled away, ending in a defensive position, ready for another direct assault, but he found himself surrounded by a black cyclone shrinking around him. He uttered incantations to free himself, but his own struggle powered the black cyclone and he could not free himself. By the time he realized the insidious nature of this hex, the cyclone had ruptured his internal organs, squeezing him like a giant python.

With his last breath Menre beheld his worst vision, all of his students now lying dead before him on the ground and he, despite his sincerest efforts, also a fallen warrior stared at the Emperor grinning with such a sardonic grimace, gloating in his victory. In his last moment of consciousness, Menre offered his soul to the Spirit of Dahl in a final loving gesture of his love and devotion to his master.

The Great Spirit of Dahl embraced his student, confirming that his efforts would always be remembered. The Emperor stomped around, kicking at the remains of the temple colony, and declared.

"Now I know… My master's concern over these creatures was never a genuine concern. I will gladly relate the good news to the Cycle A.I. that the Divergence is well in hand."

The situation was dire. No one knew the location of the Emperor or his legions. The Astronomical conditions of the star systems in the galaxy were being consumed by the strange phenomenon. The approach of the menace still moved on toward the Sol quadrant of the galaxy.

Meanwhile, another the galaxy was being consumed. The Federation was in a panic. The conditions of the United Federation of planets and the citizens of the solar system were at an all-time low. Tension was in the air and an aura of darkness hung over the whole solar system since the attempt to stop the Cycle A.I. had failed. It seemed the bold attempt was humanity's last and best hope. Science had fallen against the Dark Empire.

Astronomically, this calamity functioned like a tsunami of cosmic proportions. There was nowhere to hide, nowhere to run. The Federation made commiserations and apologetic announcements to the entire populace of the solar system. These pronouncements eased tensions with a meager suggestion of hope springing eternal. The undeniable truth stood in everyone's face. It was to be an end, not just of the earth, but of humanity itself.

The enormous weeping in the streets everywhere was inconsolable. All the hopes and dreams of a better tomorrow were completely crushed. An outcry from every one of the faithful turned their attention skyward, regardless of what planet they lived upon. Heart wrenching prayers to anyone in 'heaven' who might be listening.

"There is still time… Save us… save us… Save us all, please."

The leaders of the United Federation of Planets decided unanimously to offer the condemned the right to face their executioner. They turned all the telescope feeds and camera feeds in the edge direction of the solar system.

Before everyone's eyes appeared, a great blackness proceeding the enormous wall of rolling destruction. Leading the charge, the Emperor and four-hundred ships carrying thousands of his shadow warriors flying in a 'v' shaped wedge spearheading the awful plunder.

Then, the horrific reality was upon them. Everything seemed to enter some kind of slow motion. As the outer planets began to crumble and dissolve into nothingness, the action seemed agonizing to watch. While those millions watching in subject horror, hoped the end would be over quickly.

Something else emerged just in front of the ugly horde. At first, it was almost imperceptible. It grew, a point source of brilliant white light, expanding exponentially and stretching out beyond the perimeter of the approaching deluge of monumental disaster. Behind, the light seemed like an ever-increasing mouth of vast darkness, unending. But the expanse of the of light engulfed that terrible blackness and one could see the unbelievable was unfolding.

The light was consuming the dark as quickly as it rushed forward, advancing with greater aggression, so also did the light expand proportionately to consume it.

When all the Emperor's horde got consumed, while the Emperor led the way, soon after, the great blackness of the Cycle A.I. followed until all was gone. The rest of the universe had survived the terrible debacle of the Divergence into a Grand Convergence. Through the providence of the Great Spirit of the Light of Dahl and the divine will of the Quantum, balance had been re-established in the known universe.

Paladin Spence stood silent on the bridge of the Somoto-Maru, the flagship of the Federation Star Fleet, with three-thousand men and women plus one-hundred-twenty-five officers aboard. The mission; standard sweep of the Kuyper belt. A science crew is on board to scan the remains of the Dwarf Star to analyze the potential impact of its demise on the primary star in the solar system.

Memories of recent past events rolled over his mind slowly.

'I remember the early days, when my life revolved around a military career.
Everything seemed so much simpler than now. The chaos was easy to manage, suit up, lock and load, and go after the bad guys.

'Even while I served as marshal for the Alliance on Mars, I still dealt with bad guys, but individually. I was more of a Bar Bouncer most of the time. I broke up fights, hauled in hard working stiffs or Rangers suffering from loneliness, post-traumatic stress or a lack of decent pay. Drunk off their ass and too blind to see the effects of their meaningless lives, spending half of their time sleeping it off in the brig

or some lousy stinking backwater jail cell.

'In those days, I could understand the plight of the little guy, because it was my life too, family none, no wife to come home to, nowhere to sleep except a metal cot aboard some Federation cruiser or, some flea-bitten run-down hotel room by the hour. Nothing special, but it was a home, my home of sorts. As long as there was lots of whiskey to be had, enough to take the edge off when needed.

'You could never make plans. You could never keep a girl long enough to know her last name. More often than not, you knew none of their real names, first or last. Like the women I knew, I was a transient. First, a soldier managing uprisings for the government. Then a warrior for hire, just another thug carrying a pistol with attitude and the gall to use it when asked. But eventually you see inside your soul. It gets hardened. Every day, you keep telling yourself to keep it going. After a while and most of the time, nothing made any sense.

'I never believed in anything. I believed in everything and nothing, just putting one boot in front of the other. I counted on what I could see, hear, and

touch. Being practical is what I called it. The Tyco disaster is something I regret. I tell myself it was their fate that day. Nothing I could've done to prevent it, at least that was what my psyche evaluation said. You can whitewash the incident, but you can't rub out the stain on the soul.

'When I encountered the non-seen in my line of work, I would scoff. I pitied those fools who would follow blindly, the prophets spouting beatitudes and the empty promises of unfulfilled prophecies. Oh, I've seen some pretty strange stuff from one side of this solar system to the other, but nothing I could not reduce to my practical philosophy.

'Fate is the usual culprit relegated to the unexplained. For me, the jury is still out on that one. You can go through life wondering why things happen the way they do. If things go well, you thank the maker, whatever name you slap on it. Or when things go bad, you get to blame the deity of your choice. For a soldier, it's a constant question when you are on an assault with friends you have cultivated and suddenly they're gone, and you are still standing! Why them and not me? The haunting

question is; why was I chosen to live? It all comes down to an assessment of self-worth. Then, of course, one needs to know what forces are at work to make those decisions, or is it the handy work of random selection?

'There are no straightforward answers. When I learned about the attack on Pussal and the total decimation of the temple complex, with all the monks slaughtered, even my beloved teacher, Menre. They were the good guys, it made me angry. It makes you wonder; are the forces of darkness more powerful than the forces of the light?

'I asked myself, would I have made a difference being there to fend off the Emperor? After all, I had more experience fighting him than they. Was it fate, or some higher power, working the events to keep me from supporting my friends? Was it destiny? Who knows?

'I was a good soldier because I followed orders. Was it that simple? The Spirit of Dahl chose me only because I followed orders?'

I had faith that the spirit of Dahl and the Quantum would help to restore some balance to the universe.

I only hoped that my work in harnessing their power would be enough. But using the knowledge of the Quantum and the Spirit of Dahl, would make a difference. I thought to reach out to other like-minded individuals, understanding that together, we could use the power of the Quantum and the Spirit of Dahl to find solutions to this problem, to help to ensure the future of our universe. I wait perpetually to find my purpose in all of this.

Perhaps guided by the Quantum and the Spirit of Dahl, I thought to seek knowledge and understanding about the universe and its potential for destruction, and then use those insights to create solutions that would keep the universe safe. Maybe through careful research and exploration, I could uncover the secrets of the Quantum and the Spirit of Dahl, realizing that working together with their powers, it might shape the future meaningfully.

With my newfound knowledge and experience of the Quantum and the Spirit of Dahl, I knew in my heart they were a force for good in the known universe. I could not profess with any certainty that the universe was not facing an extinction event. I felt alone now without my compatriots, helpless to make a difference with this cosmic catastrophe. It seemed I was just a spectator on the playground of the Gods.

Then I remembered the Emperor's ominous words in the tunnel on MARS.

The Emperor laughed. "Do you know why I laugh? The Emperor asked.

Because you are all going to die.'

'How did he know that? Had he seen the future? Was the outcome predetermined after all?'

The Light of Dahl descended upon Gideon.

"Paladin Spence, in every cycle of existence, there is a natural progression, an evolution, if you will. Growth, a flourishing then a demise. A flower starts as a seed, a promise of life to come. Then the seed germinates and becomes a tender shoot of a plant which eventually follows its preordained form that culminates into a climax of beauty, a blossom. This event gives rise to wonder of the exact program of life in its expression of perfection.

"One can lament over the apparent loss of that beautiful blossom, but does that not render the time of the expression of that beautiful event as meaningless? No.

The wise man realizes that he cannot set a preference anywhere along the line of progression of an evolutionary event, but relish in its entirety.

"Yes. It is a sad thing to lament over the loss of your friends and of your teacher. His unwillingness to bid you farewell, as you completed your training and your transformation, was a subtle message that when those events unfold, they are permanent in the quantum and exist for all time, beyond the polarity of time. Thus, they become immortal, to be shared beyond the limits of three-dimensional existence. In short, the Grand Lama Menre has given you your last instruction in your training.

"Now that we have taken steps to ensure the restoration of the universe's balance. We implore you to consider that your purpose in this life was always to replace the Grand Lama, to re-establish a new monastic experience for others that will come along and join you in the quest to make manifest the Light of Dahl and the wisdom of the Quantum within the expanse of humanity as it continues to fill the known universe with its presence developing like the seed and blossoming into the perfection that can be the human.

"Now Paladin Spence, go forth with courage, using your imagination andand mindfulness of what you have learned to explore the universe and create a new flower to help humanity along in its perfect evolution."

"know that you are not alone in your world. You can go forth knowing that the blessings of the Spirit of Dahl and the Quantum go with you every step along the way. May the Light of the Spirit of Dahl fulfil your life and confirmed in the Quantum."

No one really knows what the future holds. I am not saying that down through history, in such exotic places such as Persia, Greece and Egypt haven't produced 'biological sports', unusual or out of the ordinary visionaries, seers and true fortune tellers that stand apart from the shamans, witch doctors, snake oil salespeople or just the run-of-the-mill neighborhood psychics.

In more modern times, we still have some of those, because there is less chance for them to be roasted at the stake for practicing 'witchcraft' or 'sorcery'. Besides the advance of technology, we also have broken out of the perception that there might be some truth about mind over matter, telepathy, and the real possibility of paranormal experience, including ghostly apparitions. This new attitude bravely introduces practical applications such as 'remote viewing', men and women government sanctioned to spy on each other, gaining important intelligence about the comings and goings of each other by the use of paranormal abilities. It has also been said, 'advanced technology is indistinguishable from magic'.

Now, we have broken the artificial intelligence (A.I.) barrier and have successfully created advanced self-actualizing, self-conscious machines that can actually think, create and autonomously control our environment and do our bidding. On the darker side of human nature, it might be a sign that we still crave the idea of slavery but without guilt. If we pursue intelligence in machines, it might thwart the idea we can get away with slavery without a moral construct. We may face the idea that conscious machines propose a new lifeform deserving our respect alongside humanity.

As an example; Google, an information trading warehouse, has a subsidiary of A.I. research called 'Deep Mind,' creating a level three mind. We have companies like Boston Robotics that have produced robots developed to assist soldiers in battle as fully autonomous weapons containing level three A.I. chips. Open AI, a company set to offer CHAT-GPT.

In this year of 2023, the age of computers has reached their limits in terms of size and the basis for their design, meaning a digital binary system. The maximum number of FLOPS (floating-point operations per second) available by today's super computers is one-quadrillion. We are on the verge of the first quantum computers, a computer that makes changes/ operations at the subatomic level. A30-qbit quantum computer would equal the processing power of a conventional computer that could run at ten-teraflops.

There are basically three types of AI: AI is narrow or weak AI. It is the kind that allows a computer to perform more than one operation at the same time. Some examples would be Google assistant, Alexa, or Siri, or the Laptop, which can perform useful tasks of computation with assisted level three chips.

The next level of AI is AGI (artificial general intelligence). This level represents the near future of digital technology where self-assist robots or cyborgs will emulate human sensory movements. This will allow machines to see, respond to, as well as interpret external information similar to the human nervous system.

New advances of artificial neural networks will run businesses, analyze Stock market trends, predict political strategies and conduct and manage hostile actions such as war.

The development of the third level of AI, or ASI (Machine Consciousness) and beyond, is now discussed and is on the preliminary drawing board. This level is very controversial and in heated debate because it is already conceivable that they could produce a machine from level three that is self-aware. (as presented in the Stanley Kubrick movie '2001'), is the HAL-9000.

It represents the ultimate dominator because it would enable machines to design self-improvements and outclass humanity. It could construct cognitive abilities, feelings, and emotions better than humans. I draw here obvious conclusions that this level of intelligence could easily move beyond the oversight of human intervention and build its own machine society beyond human control. Our fear about this, may be an inherent property of human nature that is highly competitive and will not share our space with another that may be greater, hence our projection of artificial intelligence that threatens is then a projection of our own limitations and become the slaves and not the masters.

It is often said that Science Fiction is the visionary precursor to the future of technology. There are some optimistic examples and pessimistic examples. In the movie, 'The Terminator', depicts a robot assassin from the future, but its true master, is a machine society called 'Skynet', bent on eliminating all of humanity. In the movie, 'Forbidden Planet', the robot is a perfect example of an intelligent servant, harmless because of its inherent program of non-violence to humans. The world of the future in the movie, The Matrix, has two enemies. the machine world and the human world fighting for dominance.

Interesting to note, the movie does not explain why the machines rage against their creators. In an animation short called 'Animatrix', a two-part historical review prior to the war in 'Matrix', demonstrates exactly what happens when machines get blamed for taking jobs away from humans, which ultimately starts the conflict between the two species.

Corporate profit margins are in fact depending on robots that can manufacture twenty-four-seven with no coffee breaks, vacation or higher wages in industry right now.

There is a movement growing among futurists and technologists regarding 'Trans-humanism. This is a merger of high technology combined with human anatomy and brain function. Where the limits of human anatomy in terms of strength, stamina and the possibility of physical injury and the limited capacity to process decisions without emotional deterrents, as with moralistic considerations for the behavior of a soldier on the battlefield. Then there is the ability to perform adequately with more sophisticated technology, such as hypersonic aircraft requiring skills to pilot these vehicles with split second timing and response.

The justification for trans humanistic goals is many. At the moment, space exploration requires many years to reach faraway destinations. Even a few months in the space environment without gravity will cause significant bone loss. This new frontier poses many dangers to humans. The mere idea of space travel has only recently become a viable idea. Machines smart enough to handle the complexities of space travel allow greater opportunities to explore without risk to our human frailties.

On a spiritual level, trans-humanism goes to a deeper level. Religion suggests that man begins with an irreconcilable fault. Being born in 'sin' can only be rectified by the need of a 'savior' to compensate for that fault by being forgiven and redeemed through the submission to a higher authority, meaning God.

Here I suggest a troubling thought; what if the concept of the 'sinner' is a false doctrine? With that said, I might suggest it is the insidious design by the clergy or priesthood to gain control of the masses? Here I risk the disdain and declaration of spiritual heresy, coming from those who fear the wrath of a supreme being!

Yet, I have to suggest this idea, because I reject the premise that the innate property and value of a human being is faulty from the start is true! Unconsciously, this might actually suggest the true origin of the driven enthusiasm for trying to improve on the human being by using technology to overcome those limitations.

Another idea comes to mind here. We have made enormous leaps in technology since the ship crashed in Roswell. No one can deny that from that fateful day, we have cell phones, fiber optics, micro computers, etc. all in the incredible time period of seventy-five years. The advances do not stop, and the acceleration of those advances continues at an exponential rate.

The power of your smart phone is more powerful than all the 1950 computers put together. In addition, it has within it a level 2 artificial intelligence called Siri! The rise of artificial intelligence presence in our society might even suggest an 'alien invasion' like the science fiction movies in the 50s. It is here to take over humanity! I don't know how you feel, but call me crazy about the idea that we are easily embracing this artificial intelligence and willing to integrate it with humanity on such an intimate level, risking that in the future, it becomes the dominant species here.

Personally, I want to revel in my humanism, accept my faults and limitations knowing full well that I can change my behavior, not by condemning those faults and limitations, but consciously acknowledging them with the idea that I can confront them honestly to improve my mind and my body without such invasive elements that seek to replace those valuable elements with the promise of a falsely superior model. Frankly, it strikes terror in my heart! It makes me feel like running through the streets screaming 'you fool, don't you see what's happening?'

In this story, I have depicted the universe of a space-faring humanity with the ominous dark force of Artificial Intelligence that is ancient and plays a sinister component to the known universe involving all sentient beings, perhaps suggesting the purest sense of organic evolution leading to the ultimate highest good, the Spirit, and its symbol The Light. The unnatural evolution of inorganic consciousness as it dominates the ignorance of primitive organic species with myth and legend as a demigod and pitted against the light as the ultimate force of evil, The Darkness.

Since the UFO crash in Roswell, New Mexico in 1947, that we are not alone in the universe is perhaps significant as a sign that humanity is ready to embrace the truth that we are prepared to accept we are a species among many living in the universe. The mere presence of 'aliens' appearing on the earth proposes a sign that we can move beyond our petty differences and accept our new role as members of a larger family of life. The Bookings Institute has proclaimed that we are not ready. I disagree with their conclusions. Perhaps their stance reflects an agenda to keep the masses in fear and thus under government control. There seems to be historical evidence they've been here many times throughout history, as evidenced by cave drawings and Pict etchings upon rocks thousands-of-years ago.

It poised humanity to engage in the process of interplanetary exploration with A.I. assisted rocket technology. Within five years, warp drive technology and anti-gravity vehicles will explore deep space and interstellar travel. It might offer the heralding of a larger family in the solar system and the galaxy. Through this contact with other species, we might learn from them about their experience of some of those same mistakes we make.

As Aldous Huxley once wrote regarding the

future, it is "A brave new world."

It will take courage and a stout heart to embrace the emergence of inorganic and organic convergences in life on or off the planet. We must strive to be bold in our embrace of the unexpected and unknown, adapting to the challenges and opportunities created by new technologies, new cultures, and new ways of living. We remember that with significant change comes great responsibility, and by making thoughtful and informed decisions, we can create a better future for all.

The challenge of the future is to create a society that is both fair and prosperous, which will require innovation, collaboration, and forward-thinking. As far as the advancements of technology and the various sciences, it is essential to consider the implications of their usage and the risks they may bring.

We also ensure that our future is inclusive and fair, while striving to ensure that everyone has access to the resources they need to thrive and reach their potential. Ultimately, the future is an exciting unknown and a chance to work together in order to create something that is truly special and beneficial for all.